Out of What Chaos

Out of What Chaos
A Novel

Lee Oser

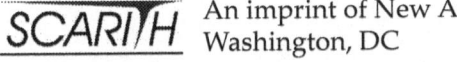 An imprint of New Academia Publishing
Washington, DC

Library of Congress Control Number: 2006939151
ISBN 978-0-9787713-4-8 paperback (alk. paper)

 An imprint of New Academia Publishing
P.O. Box 27420 - Washington, DC - 20038-7420

 NEW ACADEMIA PUBLISHING | info@newacademia.com
www.newacademia.com

I say this prayer for them
That the sun's bright strength shall break out
Wave on wave of all the joy
Life can give, across their land.

Aeschylus, The Eumenides

To Kate

Contents

ONE
Portland

The house was furnished with the lonely appurtenances of a widow. There were a black console piano and a glass bookcase with some musty books. The hard years lingered in the desolate symmetry of couch and chairs, in the raw artifice of living arrangements, cheery but awful. The genius of the house was a miniature stuffed dog, salt-and-pepper in coloring, a Shih Tzu, I believe, who resided on the piano. He died unexpectedly during the Clinton era, and the widow was unable to part with him. A canine rictus suggested that in some sphere things had gone well. It was a gratuitous, slightly crooked smile, bordering on a salacious leer, though whether a parting grace or an artful flourish I find it difficult to say. An emerald collar adorned the neck with an engraved silver bell that said:

Jim Dandy
Part of the Family

Hank occupied the bedroom in the house proper, leaving the two rooms in the trailer. We had single beds, pine dressers, little windows with cranks, and a bathroom with a jerrybuilt shower. The shower leaked a waltz. The carpet throughout the house was crisp and thin, and much the same aquamarine as the felt on a pool table. Our practice room, when we bought new amplifiers, was the trailer's living room. During rehearsals we looked directly into the kitchen, where the cabinets had a bleached, warped appearance. The linoleum floor, drained by the western exposure, had undergone a gradual transition from eggshell white to mummy yellow.

That first evening the three of us sat on the rug, drinking beer. We had our instruments in hand, twanging away and staring at the enormous future. Jim Dandy reclined quietly on the sofa. We placed a wooden match in his mouth, to appease his spirit.

"My dad's pissed," Hank said, tapping his drumsticks. "He keeps asking when I'm going back to college."

"I suppose it's natural," I said. "People just expect their kids to go to college."

I never met Hank's parents. They lived in a gated community near Seattle. The farm, he explained, had been left them by an elderly relative, someone he met when he was small, someone he couldn't remember. He pointed with a stick to a watercolor above the sofa.

"That's her," he said. "Esther."

I observed the flawless execution of the signature. It was an amateurish painting of Mount Hood in a lavender sky, with faint streaks of cloud and a gangly bird. Hank said the artist died a fortnight before they found her. He sniffed the air significantly.

"How are your parents?" he said.

Rex got up and returned with a book: a hardcover copy of *Women and Chaos* by Penelope Driver. Hank read aloud the handwritten dedication on the inside cover.

To my dear friends Rex and Friedrich. Love, Penelope.

"How is it?" he asked.

"It's been widely reviewed," I told him.

He continued into the opening paragraph.

The death of God was long ago. The reign of Man is over. The West is now a void. Romantics and reactionaries persist, but the armies of thought do not rally under their banner.

Why then are we living the future of a dead past?

"*No comprendo,*" he said.

Penelope Driver is an expert on the psychology of chaos. She grew up near Scarsdale, the only child in a Dutch mansion. Her father, the aspirin magnate, maintained a stable of horses for her. An indiscretion on the night of her eighteenth birthday doomed the family fortune, when a scientist from Driver and Driver toppled from her balcony into the garden below, where my grandmother fired him on the spot. Before shooting himself in the ear he laced an entire shipment of Driver's Remedy with strychnine. The business never recovered.

"Mom's a genius," Rex said.

"The West...Does she mean California?" Hank asked.

"Probably," I said.

For a few punctual weeks I bussed tables at Maximilian's Restaurant on NW 23rd Avenue. Then my boss and I had a falling out. I was cleaning up the empty lounge after lunch when he shuffled over to the bar. Mr. Harold Kane was sixtyish, plump and bald. He always wore a jacket and a tie. The fountain and its floodlight were on, and a bright jet of water splashed and chuckled on the dolphin's back as I went about my lowly task. In the shadow of the fountain I became aware of Mr. Kane's eyes darting to and fro. He crept softly behind, put a hand on my back, and said I was doing a fine job.

"There might be an opening for a waiter next week."

"That would be great."

His hand paused on the small of my back. I could see white spikes of hair, like hog's bristles, protruding from his nostrils. Then he squeezed my right buttock as if he was inspecting grapefruit.

"Fuck off," I said.

"Sorry."

When I left work that afternoon, Mr. Kane trotted windily onto the sidewalk after me.

"Look, Freddie," he said, dabbing his forehead with a silver handkerchief. "You can have the waiting position. No hard feelings, okay?"

Rex and Hank found the episode to their taste. They demanded a full account, asking if I'd gone "for a dip in the fountain." Then Hank opened a can of lager and raised it high in salute.

"Bottoms up!" he said.

In his drollery he spit the beer in a spray of foam onto the carpet, where it sank like sea scum.

"Boy," Rex said, "that's what I call raising Kane."

"Fuck you, Rex."

"No *hard* feelings..."

They suffered convulsions of mirth. They doubled over, slapped their thighs, and crumpled to the floor. They rolled on their backs and beat the carpet with their fists.

When I telephoned my sister, Ellen, she told me to forget about it.

"Change jobs if you feel uncomfortable. You need to let it go."

"But he put his hand on my ass."

"Let's hope he washed it afterwards."

She mentioned that my brother-in-law was running for office.

"Why would he do that?"

"Today he's mad at trial lawyers."

"But you're lawyers yourselves."

"Everyone in California's a lawyer," she said. "All the Lord's people."

A classified ad in the *Oregonian* asked for a lunch waiter at Kilroy's Tavern. By night it was a landmark of the Portland music scene. By day it served the needs of a few dozen working-class guys, a remnant of the pre-tech economy. They wore heavy black boots with steel toes and carried bunches of keys on their thick belts. There was a stage upstairs and a stage downstairs. They were just wooden platforms, no curtains, with a few adornments but no lighting or PA system. Upstairs a bugle hung on the wall over the piano. A blushing gnome with a wreath of paper flowers garnished the stage downstairs, alongside a metal Christmas tree strung with green lights. We served lunch upstairs between the bar and the dance floor. It was a modest, straightforward operation, with ten small round black tables, each with its complement of condiments and an ashtray.

The lady who hired me was a strict Roman Catholic. Mrs. Gruda went to church every morning at seven o'clock. She kept a sign in the kitchen that said "Coincidences are spiritual puns." We used to discuss God and it alarmed her to learn I'd never been baptized. After a few weeks her husband came to refer to me as the young pagan.

"Would the young pagan please clean the rest rooms?"

Mr. Gruda had joined the Army–"snuck into the war" was his phrase–at the ripe young age of sixteen and caught the last phase of the Pacific Campaign. He took part in the invasion of Okinawa, on April 1, 1945. He said out there on the island they used to get tanked on Aqua Velva aftershave and fruit juice. It could make you go blind.

In his early seventies Mr. Gruda was still hale if a little weak in the eyes. His wife was ten years younger, an agile old hen. They had five children. She made the lunches and he worked the bar.

If it was slow, sometimes Mr. Gruda had me sit down and read the paper to him. He was particularly fond of natural disasters. I would indulge him with a story about an earthquake or a tidal wave to which he devoted his undivided attention, occasionally summoning Mrs. Gruda. When the big flood came he was simply agog. There was a town whose cemetery was inundated and the coffins floated out. Mr. Gruda called for Mrs. Gruda immediately. The ghoulish fleet was spotted twenty miles downstream, caskets breasting the tide, pushing south. Mrs. Gruda listened solemnly. She bowed her head. It seemed she was revolving a fine point of theology.

"It's the expensive ones that float," she decided. "The cheap ones sink to the bottom."

"But pine would float," he said.

"Only for a moment, dear. Then it would just fill with water and sink to the bottom. You'd be stranded."

"Hmm, that's true," he reflected.

On the subject of our involvement with Iraq, Mr. Gruda had one comment.

"Saddam the Sodomite."

"That's enough," Mrs. Gruda clucked.

I must have heard it a hundred times.

The Grudas built Kilroy's Tavern in 1960, the year they were married. It returned to them like a lovestruck elephant as one entrepreneur after another failed to make the rent: and they always renamed it Kilroy's Tavern. The Grudas' youngest son, Jack, was the force behind the bar's night life. He slept until noon and showed up around three.

We received an unexpected letter from our father's third wife, Ursula, whom we referred to variously as "The Trophy," "Gold Cup," and "Feather Bed." She wrote to say we'd been right after all.

At twenty-five Les Fontane envisioned a future in politics. He'd been a handsome scholarship boy in the Jesuit schools who showed every sign of promise. His own father, Les senior, worked fifty years selling tennis rackets and golf clubs in the Empire State Building. When Les married Penelope he had bigger plans. He turned down an offer from a major brokerage and struck out on his own. He named his first son Rex and dreamed of an empire to rival his father's hundred stories. But his true vocation was white-collar crime. Just before our parents divorced he was indicted for dealing false information. Penelope moved us from New York to Palo Alto, and Les's peers found him guilty on one count of obstruction of justice.

After six months in the pen, he tried his hand at real estate. He moved a thousand properties in five years. He bought a big silver Benz, joined the Downtown Athletic Club, and married a gold-digger from Buffalo. That summer after high school Les was out of the slammer and back in the saddle. His magnificent freedom wouldn't last, but when he invited his sons back east to learn about business, he was brimming with friendly advice—until we got into a squabble over finances. He quoted Emerson and preached the virtues of self-reliance. Real men, he said, didn't need "helping out." The very phrase signaled the decline of American culture.

Ursula sided with Les and the Sage of Concord. Now she was writing to say they'd bilked her too. The daughter of a machinist, she'd had her dainty paws on twenty rooms with servants. Everything slipped away and there was no money left. It stood to wonder, did she want us to send her some? She signed "love and kisses" and enclosed a photo of herself with her stepchildren. It was taken poolside and she was wearing a fuchsia bikini. We sat behind her, smirking.

All through college she'd been the polestar of my nightly fantasies. I couldn't escape my urgent desire to possess her, body and soul. It was my family romance. Each morning I woke with a sticky wad of kleenex littering the floor, a garland of nights dedicated to Ursula. Sometimes I neglected to remove those rose buds and they gathered dust. Now I drew a circle next to her head and in it scribbled, "Will fuck for a big house." Rex thumbtacked the picture on the wall above his amp.

Jack Gruda hadn't shown up and I was cleaning the tables down-stairs when Mr. Gruda shouted for me to open the basement door. Standing in the stairwell was a handsome young man. He wore a black leather jacket, tight black pants, and a cool striped shirt of purple and orange. He needed to set up his gear for a show. I moved a few tables to clear a path and introduced myself. I asked if he wanted help.

"Sure," he said in a husky voice. "I'm Johnny D."

Out on the street his bandmates were hauling equipment out of an old US mail van. I took a pair of drum cases and left them lumbered with the bass amp. Downstairs Johnny D was adjusting the gnome.

"What kind of music do you play?"

"Actually quite loud," he answered, picking at the wax in his ear.

"What do you call yourselves?"

"We're The Hit Men," he said, flicking away the wax.

"Oh," I said appreciatively, "*you're* The Hit Men."

He nodded and remarked that the opening act had canceled. He couldn't find a replacement on such short notice. So I mentioned that I had a band. When he heard that we'd played a few bars in San Francisco, opening for Camper Van Beethoven and other luminaries, he invited us to fill in.

"What do you call yourselves?"

Our college name was "The Dicks." It had taken a lot of abuse and I'd been sifting through alternatives for more commercial appeal.

"Rex and The Brains," I said.

The most important person we met in those first few months amidst a series of gigs opening for The Hit Men, The Slits, Film at Eleven, Isis, The Throbbing Membranes (later just The Membranes), Theater of Sheep, The Nightshades, Ed and The Boats, The Confidentials, The Unreal Gods, The Stiffs, The Shakes, The Warts (The Warts were great), Whoroboros, The Members, Napalm Beach, Obnoxious Farthead, The Lips, Sonic Halo, The Cosmic Will, Blood Hour, Totem, Slum, The Hell Cows, Jesus Presley, The Malchicks, Doghead, and Zuzu's Petals was a tall thin man with a pale scrunched face, anemic blond hair, and slate eyeballs that clicked and caromed around a room in a virtuosic display of synchronized nervousness. His name was Ed Smith.

He first approached us downstairs at Kilroy's. We knew the inky rag he published. It cluttered the windowsills of bars and night-clubs on both sides of the river. He kept showing up at our gigs. Then one night I found him deep in conversation with Rex.

"I think you guys are really good," Ed Smith said, nodding and taking a big drag on his cigarette.

He had a perpetual wince about him, as if someone had recent-ly kicked him in the balls. He exhaled a funnel of smoke and tapped his boot. His eyes clicked and caromed.

"I was saying to Rex you guys should let me manage you. I'll put your picture on the front cover of the magazine and get you some headline gigs."

"Do you manage any other bands?" I asked.

"I manage The Horny Fellows."

We liked The Horny Fellows. For one thing they played good hard rock. Direct and very effective. For another their girlfriends were strippers who danced in cages when The Horny Fellows per-formed. Likewise direct and very effective.

"Ed wants fifteen percent of whatever we earn," Rex informed me.

I drank my beer and paid close attention. Ed Smith had ap-proached Rex because he was the front man. But it wasn't exactly Rex's band, and that was a fine point.

"I've been trying to make something happen for years," Ed Smith said, offering us cigarettes. "I know I should quit. It kills you in the end. But for now I guess it keeps me going. Call me if you like."

He flicked off a pair of business cards. "Edward V. Smith. Pub-lisher and Agent."

Rex landed a job waiting tables at an upscale restaurant called The Matterhorn. There he met some cooks and a dishwasher who were also musicians. They had a band called The Lords of The West.

One night The Lords showed up at our place. They drank a case or two of beer in an hour. Then they strapped on our guitars, usurped Hank's drums, and performed a Frank Sinatra song called "Strangers in the Night." If you don't know it's a romantic ballad, and for the length of a verse they performed it pretty faithfully. They then exploded into a wailing bit of punk dementia, which ended as abruptly as it had started. And so it went: ballad, dementia, ballad, dementia, ballad, until dementia finally battered down the gates, set fire to the town, raped the women, and pushed the old people into the sea. The Lords' front man was an obese perspiring tenor named John Beazler, who stuffed himself into a pair of white barrel-waisted tennis shorts. We opened a bottle of Southern Comfort as the Lords ran off a warped little set, which they extended that evening in order to "bring up a dear, dead friend." It was Jim Dandy on maraca.

They trafficked in oldies which they anatomized, dismembered, and abused with impressive sangfroid. They were intent on the perfect synthesis of badness and perfection. The other guys left the showmanship to Beazler. I watched with fascination as they went about their work, like automobile workers assembling a shining lemon. The lead guitarist, a dishwasher named Frank, had arrived wearing a black eye patch; but he abandoned it during his first solo, a flawless surf guitar. The bassist, a gifted dwarf named Barnabas, shouted Scripture during the break-down on "Satisfaction." Stan the drummer had lost an arm to a shark, but you could close your eyes and still hear it, he never missed a beat. They were an impressive composite. Without Beazler, though, they wouldn't have been The Lords of The West. He was their Moses and their Caesar. I once heard somebody mention their original name, their name before he took the helm. They used to call themselves Fake Vomit.

Beazler was introducing "the house band."

"Ladies and gentlemen, all the way from California, where scientists are desperately searching for them...I've just received a call from Colonel Parker and he assures me they're good American boys...they wouldn't hurt a fly unless it had money...I just met these boys and let me tell you it's been frightening...no, seriously, it's been really scary. Would you please give up the love for Sexy Rexy and the Mind Benders."

Rex plugged in his Telecaster and performed by himself. He set to work on a lonely blues, delivering the vocal with effortless control, pulling back to let his voice fade, returning with an eerie falsetto. The Lords sat enthralled as he finished, descending like a prophet from heights of sapphire and sacred fire. When the last note sounded Beazler led them in a wild dance, with Hank pounding away on the tom-toms and Rex howling into the microphone.

I took the Southern Comfort out on the porch. There I found myself staring at the shadowy cattle. The howling surged into the open field and rolled down to the river. It beat against the herd like rocks. They stood motionless, huddling under the full moon, alert to the sound of their ancient enemy. I could scarcely see them they were so dark.

Returning to the kitchen in a mist of alcohol I found twelve burning eyes directed at me. Eleven burning eyes and six flushed, drunken faces. The cacophony had ended. Did they want me to say something, a shot of nonsense to finish off the evening?

"Hey diddle diddle," I thought to myself. "The cat and the fiddle, something jumped over the moon..."

"The little dog laughed!" Beazler shouted, his lips carved in a grotesque mask, his eyes aglint.

Rex shook with laughter and Beazler started barking and swiveling his bulbous head. It was strange but so were a lot of things and I didn't want to dwell on it. Sometime later I woke in total darkness, grasping after one last thought, which carried me off with it like a log on a black river: they must have had Jim Dandy in mind.

TWO
The Black Pearl

Among the male devotees of Rex and The Brains was a skinny
sleepy-eyed stripling known in the vernacular as Weez. He didn't
seem to mind being called that. Hearing himself summoned he
gave you the impression it was better to be called something than
nothing. "They call me the Weez," he'd say. When you got to know
him, he showed a fine patience with the stubborn side of life, the
missed exit, the blown tire, the street with no name, until you began
to suspect that "Weez" was the sign of some incomprehension in
others, a cry in the wind as they sped by.

He would make his entrance trailing a gang of aging adoles-
cents who'd gone to high school together and now adopted us as
their social ritual. They paid full price at the door. They groomed
themselves with brash ineptitude. They exuded a musky, goatish
charm as they applied their constitutional right to assemble at a bar
and suck a keg dry. Sometimes, late in the evening, when alcohol
loosens the chains of the spirit, one of them would begin listing
and then topple unceremoniously from his barstool. I could see it
happening while I played the bass. And it touched me with melancholy.

Weez himself was quiet and undemanding, a minor figure in
everybody's book. He was good at remembering names.

"Humans," he used to say, "are quite smart animals."

Our friendship reached the point of having a pint together. We
discussed The Three Stooges, the classic "Curly" period, of which
we were both aficionados. One evening he broached the idea of his
working for the band. He said he knew about sound and lights.

We were rehearsing when I heard the crunch of wheels on
the gravel.

"It's only that guy Weez," I said. "He wants to roadie for the band."

Our visitor ushered us out onto the driveway. Evidently he had something important to show us. Then he pointed at the side of his van, where our name was freshly painted in black uncial letters. It was a name that enchanted us wherever it appeared, a poster on a telephone pole, the heady print of a newspaper column, the graffiti on a wall. On the canine analogy, the name of the band is the scent of scents. But in this instance we met with a stranger love than any we had known. Underneath the logo Weez had painstakingly detailed a side view of the human brain: cerebrum, medulla oblongata, and other gray parts, a mirror to nature. Above it rested a crown that faced front, so that the brain appeared to be sporting its headgear sideways.

We gazed awhile in wonder.

"It's kick-ass," I said, recalling myself. "I love it."

Rex picked up some acorns from the ground. I suppose there must have been an oak nearby, though I myself have always been weak on trees. I think of Adam, scampering up the Tree of Knowledge (or was it the Tree of Life?) and refusing to come down when God wanted him in the cool of the day. Adam and his famous monkey imitations, which were fresh at the time and came so naturally to him.

"Ee-ee-ee!"

Hank walked back into the house without a word. I thought he might be going to fetch his camera.

"It's definitely kick-ass," I said.

"Why the hell is Hank using the bathroom in the trailer?" Rex asked. "Why doesn't he use his own fucking bathroom?"

I said, "It's his house."

"Get out of my bathroom, you big fuck!" Rex shouted through the window.

"Fuck you!" Hank shouted.

Rex started throwing acorns, slinging them sidearm, rapping them off the bathroom window.

"Is that a golden bottle cap?" I said.

"It's a crown," Weez replied coolly, as a helmeted acorn whizzed against the aluminum trailer, ricocheted off the van, and tapped him on the thigh. "Don't you college boys know that Rex means king? It's what you call a *rebus*."

"What's a rebus?" Rex wondered, wiping his hands.

"You know," Hank said upon his return, "like if a squirrel bites you."

"No," Weez said, sure of himself. "That's rabies."

Now that Weez was helping us haul our equipment the van became a familiar sight around the clubs. Its picture even appeared in the coveted pages of *Willamette Week*. But envy never sleeps for long in this life. To sketch the event as best as I can, somebody took a fine camel hair brush, dipped it in a can of waterproof paint, color fire-engine red, and inscribed in mock-uncial, straight in the middle of the gray matter, the four fiery letters that compose the word SUCK.

Man were we furious.

The foul deed occurred between 10:00 pm and 2:00 am on a Thursday evening, when we were competing in a battle of the bands at the old Metro on SW Burnside. We finished second behind The Hit Men. We called the police and they arrived a little before 3:00 am. It was cold and damp and foggy. The streetlamps lit the streets like greasy flares. Moisture beaded on the bricks and forked in nail-thin rivulets onto the sidewalk. Occasionally a streetcorner hosted a desolate drunk. They were setting like planets.

The police seemed disgusted with life in general and us in particular. They heard us out with scarcely a grunt. Dull of eye and stiff of limb they appeared not to have finished thawing.

"Isn't there anything you can tell us?" Rex said, shivering in the halo of a streetlamp.

"Whoever did it probably planned ahead," the cop said.

His head bobbed slightly as he spoke; but his partner conserved his energy. He might be out of fuel, I thought. Or he might be a body-snatcher. Or he might be named Joe, a relic of the Old World, of peasants from the hill country who had ended lost in America, deaf to the overtures of the sun, blind as the moon, leaden at nightfall, buried under a marble cross, and to whom he now paid unwitting homage.

"Can't you take fingerprints?" I asked.

"No," said the first cop, the livelier one. "No prints."

"What, is that your department motto? *No prints?*"

"You boys oughta be more careful where you park."

"More careful where we park!" Rex exclaimed. "As if it was our fault!

"Fuck...you," he coughed.

"You want to go to jail?" Joe said.

I said, "Let me get this straight. We really shouldn't have called you. Because it's late at night and there's absolutely nothing you can tell us."

Joe approached the van. He peeled off a glove, tested the paint with his index finger, and held it above his head, so that he looked like the Statue of Liberty.

"Look."

It was red at the tip.

"I can tell you the paint's still wet."

Neither of them laughed.

Not even Weez's good humor and prompt repair of the damage could expunge our sense of shame. Envy having done its work, rumor pointed immediately to Ted Shred from The Zeros. He was a likely suspect, an albino heroin addict with flaky skin whose bands always came in last. They were awful bands that never matured, like bananas that turn from lime green to bruised and speckled brown with never a moment's ripeness. When Shreddy crossed our path a few nights later he had a furtive air about him, like a rat among odors. We wanted the rat dead. But over the next several weeks Weez adopted a phrase, an odd memento of the crime, which he repeated at each and every sound check, until we couldn't help laughing at something absurd, whether in the words themselves or in his guileless birdlike inflection, I don't know.

"Suck brains, two, three," he would sing into the microphone, descending a fourth on the second word. Then he would modulate a few steps, "Suck brains, two, three. Suck brains, two, three. Suck brains."

We got to imitating it around the house when we needed to let off steam. We forgot about Shreddy, who might have been an innocent man. But when I finally asked Weez what he meant by it, he looked surprised and then stopped using the phrase altogether.

We were driving to the Black Pearl in the snow. The plan was for a quick soundcheck followed by dinner, leaving enough time to put in an appearance at Weez's parents' house. Hank and Rex pulled out ahead of us, and I went with Weez. We were heading uphill, Weez wiping the foggy windshield with his red lobster claw, Beazler asquat on the bass cabinet in the back. He was scrunched like a satellite payload. We heard the engine straining and tires spinning as they lost traction. No one spoke as the van sheered to the right. It was like entering a vortex, with the high branches sweeping past from the trees below the road. Weez downshifted and somehow caught a patch of asphalt to guide the vehicle back downhill.

We paid our visit to Weez's parents and Mr. Cove was there to greet us at the door. Family photographs decorated the hall in rows–a scintilla of evolutionary time–at the end of which hung a small wooden crucifix. Mrs. Cove rose from the couch in shapely blue jeans and a pink cashmere sweater, very friendly and relaxed. She wore black horn-rimmed glasses, like a Pan-Am secretary. The life hadn't gone out of the marriage, I could see. Weez introduced each of us to his parents and then to his sisters, who fluttered in to look at the boys. I hadn't reckoned on our road crew's having such a handsome family.

"Have you boys eaten dinner?" Mrs. Cove asked.

"I have some stew," she offered. "I never know if Timothy eats now that he's moved out."

"I eat, Mom," he laughed, patting his skinny belly.

"Well it's here if you change your minds."

We sauntered into the family room, an extension of the house that pushed out into the backyard. It smacked of suburban coziness, with an overstuffed couch and matching bean-bag chairs of creamy brown. On a card table lay a jigsaw puzzle where a lighthouse stood drenched in sunlight, with a thin margin of blue sky and a red-gold slope. The rest of the puzzle scattered and spilled onto the floor.

"The test of a good painting is whether it makes a good jigsaw puzzle," Weez said.

"Who says?" I asked.

"You learn these things from experience."

We were getting settled when Mrs. Cove arrived with a tray

of soft drinks and a big wooden bowl of popcorn. She lingered only long enough to pick up the jigsaw pieces that had fallen. The popcorn was the perfect kind I never make, white and fluffy, every kernel popped. The glasses had ice cubes in them. It was like high school when you visit a kid with nice parents. Weez sat at the card table to work on the puzzle and I pulled over the organ bench and we finished it together. He possessed a temperament suited to jigsaw puzzles. He stared at the puzzle and scrutinized the shape of the top piece on the pile.

"Sky pieces are the hardest," he reflected, turning over a blue shape like a gingerbread man.

We sat there, a couple of old puzzle hands, while the others watched the Blazers trounce the Bulls. Weez had the sky and I had the slope. Then I helped with the sky. We finished it just as the game ended: a thousand interlocking pieces.

Outside the snow was lazing into big wet flakes. It looked like half-a-foot: but the main roads weren't bad. Our worry was that without a good door the Black Pearl wouldn't have us back. The owner, an ex-fullback named Carl Schultz, was a beefy guy with a hard nose for business. He took an active dislike to a lot of bands. You could open a beer bottle with that schnoz of his.

"When there's no place to piss," he liked to say, "then it's a good show."

We weighed our chances of success.

"Ed did a good job getting the posters up."

"Yeah, they looked pretty good."

We drove soberly along. The sight of a slow bar on a frozen street seemed all too likely. It would mean no progress, an exhausting and disheartening failure.

"There's lots of traffic," Hank announced from behind the wheel.

"That's a positive sign," Rex said.

The queue at the Black Pearl stretched under the black canopy, onto the sidewalk, and down the block. Cars lined both sides of the street. The only parking was a quarter mile away. Then the snow let off. It dripped here and there from awnings and rooftops. Overhead the clouds brushed open a star.

To our satisfaction the big cavern was jammed, not just the seats and the bar, but every crook and cranny. The dance floor was a twisting knot of bodies.

"How's the war, Ed?"

"Hasn't even started."

Ed Smith sat at the bar awaiting our arrival. Now he escorted us downstairs to the dressing room. A small band of revelers sat on the basement floor in a purple alcove, drinking beer in a blue light. They smiled like psychedelic flowers. We smiled back as Ed Smith unlocked a door.

"For the band only," Ed Smith said, as the dust in the room rose to greet us, flinging its stale taste into our mouths.

He found the switch and an illuminated mirror over a long dressing table soaked the room in a silvery glow, hanging a cluster of lights from a cheval glass in the corner. The gray walls were bare. On the floor lay a tatty carpet of grayish-brown. There were no windows, only a vent with a noisy fan. A long black couch rested on rows of short legs, like a caterpillar.

"It used to be a strip club. The girls used to get ready here."

"It's all about performance, boys," Beazler said, coasting into the room and slipping something to Rex.

"Hey Ed," I called. "I thought you said 'band only.'"

"It's all right, Freddie," Rex said. "Beazler's my man."

I shot a look at Beazler, who was reclining on the couch chewing a biscuit. He wore a black denim jacket and a frayed t-shirt that left his hairy belly exposed. What kind of butterfly would he turn into?

"A lot of bitches upstairs," he said, gazing at the ceiling. "A hell of a lot of bitches."

After our first set I went out for a walk. The night air was pure and bracing after the smoky babel of the club. Down the quiet streets the snow mimicked the mountains and valleys of a new world. A dark sedan pulled up and a man and a woman got out, slowly. They reached into the back and retrieved a pair of sleeping kids. I watched from across the universe as they trudged heavily through the unshoveled walk with their children limp in their arms.

The show ended with an orgasmic encore of "Wild Thing." As I put my guitar away a smiling Carl Schultz met me with two large bottles of fancy German ale. A blonde was standing beside me. She was talking about acting in a pleasant voice and smoking a cigarette. All the men were looking at her. She had on a sheer black top over a black brassiere, very eye-catching; below the waist she wore a black miniskirt, fishnet stockings, and heels.

Over at her house music was slashing out the door into the snowy street. People kept arriving but there was no one I knew. A strobe light was flashing on the dancers. We danced and someone handed her some pills, which she shared with me. I opened a bottle of ale and we washed them down.

It was an aging house with high ceilings and a cascading chandelier. She took my hand and led us up a winding flight of stairs. Then we burst into her room, laughing the whole time.

"Why do you like acting?" I asked, after she closed the door behind us.

"Because I know what I want in life."

"And what do you want?"

"You know, people always ask me that."

By "people" she meant men. She sat on the bed and kicked off her heels. She looked extremely pretty.

"What answer do you give?" I said, putting my arm around her.

I could feel the effect of the pills, like a jet making the earth tilt.

"It's the only thing I really believe in. It's like dipping into other people's lives, you know. If you catch people at just the right moment, they're actually interesting."

"Otherwise they're not," I said, kissing her lips.

"Outside the play they're either boring or they're dead!"

She returned my kiss as the bass from downstairs vibrated the wall. She had a ripe cherry mouth and she was drunk.

"I'm going to be Juliet in the summer theater."

"From *Romeo and Juliet*?"

"Have you ever seen it?"

"Once, I think. You want to recite a few lines?"

"All right," she laughed, standing on the bed. "You have to imagine I'm on a balcony. You're below me in an orchard."

After she pushed me onto the floor she opened her legs with a brilliant giggle and teased up her skirt like a cabaret dancer, swishing her hips back and forth, showing off her garters and black panties. Then she grew serious and spoke her lines with passion.

> *What's in a name? That which we call a rose*
> *By any other word would smell as sweet;*
> *So Romeo would, were he not Romeo called,*
> *Retain that dear perfection which he owes*
> *Without that title. Romeo, doff thy name,*
> *And for thy name, which is no part of thee,*
> *Take all myself.*

She hopped down and I went straight for her crotch.

"Wow," I said. "You're fantastic."

"Hold on," she interrupted. "I'll be right back. Don't go away."

I lay on the bed as time meandered, wondering if a rose by any other name would smell as sweet. Somehow I knew that *rose*, if you play with the letters, reveals a Greek word for love, a French word for dare, and an English word for pain.

Raucous female laughter erupted in the hall. She returned with a bottle of beer and stretched alongside me. As she tinkered in silence with a button on my shirt her mood seemed to have changed again. Her eye shadow was darker, her lips redder. We kissed and she asked if I wanted to see her tattoos.

"Where are they?"

As her blouse floated off she watched me admiring the beautiful swell of her flesh. Her breast was so pale it seemed blue. She pointed at a dark crescent, the size of a quarter.

"What do you think?"

Pulling back her shoulders she uncupped her lovely tits in a theatrical *coup de grâce*. I touched the tattoo, like a child touching the moon in a storybook.

"The other's a rose bud. It's pink."

"Where?"

"Look!"

She fell backwards on the bed, baring the soft white flesh above the hem of her stocking. For a brief moment I sought the tattoo on her thigh. Her garter belt held the expensive stocking in place.

Squeezed onto the single bed, sleeping in bits, I recall her putting on some exotic music, a woman singing in a foreign language, Greek, I guess. In the dreamy hour before dawn a man came in and said some words to her. When I woke up she had gone.

Hank, lucky boy, never had to work. His parents saw to that. But there was an old lady down the road, a widow he met at the grocery store, and she got him to do things for her. He put the storm windows on her house when the weather turned cold. He shoveled her walk when it snowed. They went together to a church basement to play bingo. I spoke to the old lady a couple times on the phone. She referred to our drummer as "Henry." One day Henry came back from her house with a large green suit reeking of camphor. First it went to the dry cleaners. Then it went to the tailor for black buttons and a lustrous purple lining. It had no holes and needed only slight alterations. Finally Hank strode before us, an image of the Kings of Swing in glory before Elvis changed the world.

By winter's end Rex and I could afford to be self-employed. Even after Ed Smith took his cut, and deducting for sound and lights, as well as a small sum for Weez, we had plenty of money. Beazler took the opportunity to hang up his chef's hat. How he maintained himself at first escaped me. I was struck by the fact that, although he retired from the kitchen of The Matterhorn, he was holding court in the dining room. In the late afternoon, during what he called "business hours," he drank coffee, answered calls, and played host to a train of visitors. A credulous soul might have supposed Beazler to be riding the crest of a new wave in politics, such was the variety of faces that came and went amidst the open commerce of the day. But in reality Beazler was doing a brisk trade in cocaine. The manager of the restaurant fed his habit and watched the door. The owner remained in the dark.

On occasion Rex met with Beazler to drink coffee, check out the clientele, and test the product.

"Are you doing a lot of *crack*?" I asked.

"It relaxes me after a gig. That's all. It's under control."

While Rex had things under control I stuck to a scheme I sentimentally called *past, present, and future*. Past was having been. Present was continuing to be. Future was not starting to do coke. Rex's reassurances only confirmed my view of the subject.

One night our differences nearly broke up the band. A fan had been giving him head and he resented my intrusion. She didn't seem to mind, though. She just smiled and stood there.

"It's not crack, it's coke," he snapped.

"You're overdoing it."

He chopped the drug with a razor and snorted.

"What?" he said.

In the mirror I could see a touch of white powder on the side of his nose.

"I don't like it when you're coked up. You don't play as well."

"I don't like you in flannel," he said, appraising my shirt. "You know you've always looked shitty in flannel. Who's your fashion advisor–Kurt Cobain?"

"Fuck you, superfly."

The girl took her turn bending over the drug as Rex and I swore at each other. When the line disappeared she stood back from the dressing table, sucked in the last of it by pressing closed one nostril and then the other, and looked at us with an air of expectation verging on absence of mind. Then she combed her hair in the cheval glass.

I said, "This is it. I won't go back on unless you promise me something."

"What?"

"No more coke during the show. I won't play with you if you're coked up."

"After's fine?"

"After's fine. Just try not to overdo it, you fucking crackhead."

But afterwards I was still angry at him.

"Good evening," I told the audience. "We're Rex and The Crackheads."

Something I discovered during this period may have a bearing on the world of neuroscience. The name of the band being Rex and The Brains, a word or two about brains may possibly hold thematic interest as well. What I discovered–it can be confirmed by anyone in my peer group, say for instance Harry of The Warts–is that there are times when you can play your instrument, getting the parts perfectly straight and staying in time, when you are simply shitfaced out of your mind. A truly stupendous phenomenon. Many an evening I have stared at my fingers, flying up and down the frets like hummingbirds, and wondered what on earth they were doing. They seemed far too busy to tell me, or even to wave hello. I'm not suggesting I could have played my parts with my head dissevered from my body, though it would have been interesting to try. Now I see through a glass of beer, darkly, but then I shall see face to face. Meanwhile I can report that the brain doesn't grow in a box. It is one of those organs with reach.

Beazler told me he bought his stuff from a guy he met at one of our gigs. The guy owned a gorgeous house in the West Hills. He had a young wife and a black BMW. Then he got arrested. The busy afternoons ended at The Matterhorn.

"How are you going to survive?" I asked him.

We were in the park blocks, gathered under the colossal bronze statue of Abraham Lincoln. We were having our picture taken. As Beazler spoke I was observing him, his greasy hair the color of burnt hamburger, his malleable lips and soft quivering nose, his small blue eyes.

"I'll fight my way back," he said. "I always do."

Beazler said things mostly for their entertainment value.

"So you're fresh out of drugs."

"Not exactly. I still got a few painkillers for my friends."

His connection was sitting in the county jail of all places. He'd run into the guy's wife in the supermarket.

"I was only buying a quart of milk. She told me I might be hearing from the District Attorney. Fucking bitch."

"It isn't her fault," I suggested.

"I tell you she looked pleased about the whole thing. Like she never loved the guy."

What could I say? But Beazler was no idiot. He toyed with conversation from a long oblique angle that was really a test of the other person's intelligence. He figured he was smarter than you. He didn't really give a roasted egg what you thought so long as he was getting what he wanted.

"Maybe she's cutting a deal with the DA."

He shook his head no, like he was sampling a tart marinara.

"Maybe she's making off with the coke herself."

"No. She doesn't have the balls."

"So what do you think the reality is?"

"Reality?!" his voice leapt up a register. "Reality is whatever you can get away with. That's reality."

I still have a photograph from that session. All smiles and nobody sober at three in the afternoon. Watching over us the dignity of the bronze head is undiminished.

Sometimes we'd take in a show to find girls or keep up with the local talent. The Lords of The West were opening for The Horny Fellows at a new club called The Mediterranean in NW Portland, a ten minute drive. It was the last of the cold days and we were feeling a little stir crazy.

The Lords had a song called "A," which droned on very loudly over a single A chord. It segued into an even longer song called "C." They were being dull with a will, forcing the demands of listenability back into our faces.

"Chord changes aren't our forté," Beazler explained to the sparse audience.

He was wearing a tangerine jogging suit, XXX large, and a lime-colored baseball cap that said KNUCKLEHEAD in white letters. On a vintage gold-top Les Paul, Frank started blasting out the main riff to "Imagine" by John Lennon as Beazler rapped out lyrics on his favorite theme of sodomy. He had scrupulously crafted the rhymes. "Follow me, onto me, bonhomie, sodomy..." He strutted and leered. He flaunted his fingers like The Notorious B.I.G. He grimaced and grooved. "Dreamer, schemer, ream her, redeemer..."

"Thank you very much," he Elvised to scattered applause. "Stanley Swift on drums, Barnabas Watt on bass, Francis Malone on guitar, and I'm John Beazler, Jr. Let's have a warm round of one-handed clapping for God on air guitar..."

When Rex joined The Lords for an encore I could tell he was up to no good. It was the way he and Beazler exchanged looks on stage. The Lords delivered an overwrought lounge version of "One" by U2, with Barnabas overplaying the bass, which of course dwarfed him. Come to think of it, he might have been performing a different number altogether, maybe an Eagles song. The Eagles, I say, for whose sins California is now paying such a terrible price. I had noticed Barnabas playing two bars behind Frank and Stan; and now I am as sure as I can be, it was that lugubrious dirge entitled "One of These Nights." The band played U2 while Barnabas, chewing bubble gum, hewed remorselessly to The Eagles. Beazler vanished from the stage as the final chorus progressed with Rex wailing in falsetto like a stuck pig.

The band concluded with a grotesque tuneless tumbling of drums and guitars. Barnabas blew a pink bubble the size of a kidney as Frank and Stan stared disconsolately at the floor. Wearing sunglasses and a ox-sized leather jacket over the tangerine jumpsuit Beazler suddenly reappeared by our table.

"Posers!" he shouted, pointing at the stage. "Fucking posers!"

People had no sooner started clapping than they stopped. He had the floor to himself. He managed to take up a considerable portion of it.

"You fucking atheists! This place sucks!"

He took a deep breath, like an infant winding up for a really good howl. By now every eye in the place was on him, including Frank's.

"Sucks!!" he bellowed.

Then he noticed us.

"Well, this is an unexpected pleasure," he said suavely.

The club owner, a burly Greek named Byron, came hurtling across the dance floor like a bull. He hadn't made the connection between the leviathan in the leather jacket and the zeppelin in the tangerine jumpsuit. He grabbed Beazler by the collar and jerked him towards the door, only Beazler never budged. Then I heard Rex hymning the national anthem in a voice that sounded unctuously sincere. Byron was grappling with Beazler, struggling to escort him at arm's length, like someone trying to lasso a boulder, as my brother sang fervently to the bleachers.

Suddenly Rex stopped.

"Unhand him, you pederast," he said.

"Do me!" Beazler cried.

The Greek gathered his energy, aimed a boot at Beazler's rear end, somehow missed, and rushed the stage. Hank and I stumbled over each other to defend Rex. Soon we found ourselves wrestling on the dance floor with the owner. We had him pinned and he resorted to threats.

"Get out of my club or I'll fucking kill you. I will get my pistol and shoot you in the head."

Beazler took a moment to revert to his original tangerine and lime ensemble. As he mounted the stage to join The Lords of The West, they kicked into "Beat It" by Michael Jackson. High on the ceiling the mirror ball started whirling. It created a sea of colored dots.

Byron fumed like a god in chains.

"Get out of my club or I'll kill you...I don't care who you are...I will get my pistol and shoot you."

Rex was prancing about, assisting with the chorus.

"'Beat it, beat it, beat it, beat it...'"

Byron kept up the threats as Frank absolutely nailed the guitar solo.

Rod from The Horny Fellows and his girlfriend Connie the stripper appeared like ministering angels. They doused the disco lights, uttered soothing words, and pried away the angry Greek. To my surprise he was in tears. I guess his self-esteem was in the toilet. Connie held his hand as we fled The Mediterranean, never to return there as living men.

The day we visited Salmon Head Studio the geese were migrating north, piloting over the ranch in fluid vee formations. I took it as a good omen. The studio was in the basement of a house in SE Portland owned by a sixties legend named Keith Richter. We had some new material, half-a-dozen songs, all up tempo. The likeliest of these, "Painkiller," featured a catchy melody sung over rapid-fire changes. Rex crooned it with a deliberately flat vocal, spoke instead of singing the final verse, and ended on a hollow shriek. Hank worked up a clever rhythm for the snare and bass drum. I kept my part simple and sang back-up. Near the end of the session something roused Keith Richter from his narcotic slumbers. It was then that we discovered his genius for sounds. He dug out a dusty Marshall tube amp from a spare room so that we could get the right timbre for the guitar hook. He set it to "the Pete Townshend sound on 'Live at Leeds.'" Then he asked if he could play a rough mix for a friend of his.

Ed Smith phoned the next day. It turned out that Keith Richter's friend was an LA producer named Luke Pound.

A few weeks later we were booked in Corvallis and our living quarters were above the bar. Rex and I got into another nasty fight. One of those little shitfests that siblings are so capable of. Between sets Ed Smith introduced us to a fat man in a double-breasted suit who loved the new tracks. He smiled and shook our hands and they all went out for breakfast afterwards. Rex and I still weren't speaking, so I stayed behind. Then the girl I'd been flirting with said she needed to go and I drank myself into a stupor.

I woke at dawn with no idea where I was. There was a yellow boot. Squinting upwards I saw a man's face in a cloud. He looked very tall. He had a red beard and glinting eyebrows.

"We can't have this kind of thing, son," he said.

He waited as I tried to remember where I was. Then I asked for directions back to the nightclub, which hadn't moved from its original location around the corner.

"Come on," he said in a kindly voice. "I'll walk you over."

I stood up and clutched my stomach. It was one of those puking little pukes, not a good robust stinking bellyful of chowder, just bar food and exhaust. He stood patiently by. When I was finished he escorted me down the block.

"There's worse things than drinking too much. But you have to be more careful. You won't be a kid forever."

I must have reminded him of somebody he knew.

"Sorry."

He looked to be around forty. He wore a brown Western suit, a black string tie, and a crisp yellow shirt. His voice was unusually resonant. I thought I heard it from across the street.

"God gave you this for a reason," he said, tapping his temple with his index finger. "Pay attention to things."

When I awoke for the second time my mouth was dry as the brick that had hit me in the head. It was 1:00 pm by the kitchen clock. I was standing before the sink, ladling the water with my hand and slurping it down when Rex came in.

"Where the hell you been, boy? There's some big news."

I couldn't put together either the night before or the episode of the morning. Rex stood there grinning at me. I grinned back. The water dripped off my chin like cow drool.

"There's a record company wants to sign us. Ten albums, 1.3 million bucks."

"You're kidding."

"You need to call Ellen. I want her to look over the contract."

THREE
Into the Umbra

If a thoughtful person from a hundred years ago, say the young Eleanor Roosevelt,[1] could survey how we live, one thing would stand out. Not the death of God. Most people have always had more faith in God than in the death of God. Not iPods, cell phones, or the internet, all long foreseen—as were droids and spaceships (the words seem quaint). No, it is in affairs of the heart that the present and the past have parted company. Victorian lovers used to see the starry aeons in each other's eyes. Being a busy people we have no time to waste on stars and aeons; the most celebrated and desirable prospect, on our shrinking island, features alcohol (C_2H_6O) and sexual relations (viz. the Starr Report) in about the amount of time it takes to roast a small turkey hen (*Meleagris gallopava*).

By custom Rex and I hit hard on girls. We never exactly insulted them. It seemed most of the girls we liked were beyond insult. For them and for us it was purely a matter of establishing common interests. The long romantic rigmarole, that strained bureaucratic licensing procedure for doing what dogs do, had faded into a painless formality, like getting divorced, or simply not voting. Some might say things had become more truthful. There was never that much to talk about anyway.

When April turned the cow pasture to streaming mud, so that strange fish emerged in the marshes, Rex and I started drinking earlier in the day. We were semi-famous in Portland. A lot of people seemed to recognize us or have a sense of who we were. In a tavern out on Saint Helen's Highway we met a pair of attractive dark-haired girls with an array of elegant piercings: rings and stones for

---

[1] *Née* Roosevelt.

navel, ear, nostril, and eyebrow. The taller and thinner of the two wore rectangular glasses with red frames, stylish in their way. Like many young women she studded her tongue with steel. The stud murmured its eternal message of oral sex. But the other girl surprised me. Though she must have been twenty-one, her face had an eerie meekness like a baby's. At the same time her body spoke a grown-up language all its own. But what got me was her tongue. It was actually forked like a reptile's. She called it "tongue-splitting" and said it was a done in ancient times. I thought it slurred her speech a little.

After a boozy substanceless hour or two we drove in the soft twilight back to their house. They lived closer to town, on a nondescript side street, where a lame old man walking a black mutt waved hello to the girls, who waved back in friendly fashion. It stopped raining. There were birds chirping noisily and a full moon sagging into the sky as we trailed along behind them past a few mute bushes and across a wet lawn. Inside, we drank some wine and sat on the rug as a joint floated from hand to hand. It was strong shit, Oregon's finest. The girls encouraged us to take our shirts off, and the younger one started massaging my shoulders and back. Her name was Maya. She wore a red stone in her nostril and said she liked boys with blond hair. When we kissed I noticed how her tongue felt funny.

Rex was being very forward with Deirdre, the other girl. Her glasses were off her flushed face and I caught sight of her titties before she stood up, put her glasses back on, and dropped in a DVD. She said it was a "ritual." It occurred to me they'd been making references to rituals and religion all afternoon.

I tasted my wine, which was cool and sweet, and watched the TV. It began with a group of half-dressed people wearing masks. They were gathered in what appeared to be a warehouse or cellar with crude drawings on the walls. The whole thing put me vaguely in mind of Mardi Gras until the camera lingered on a wall painting of a red-masked face with black eye sockets and a split tongue. It didn't look like it was preparing for the rigors of Lent.

Deirdre explained they worshipped something called the "Umbra." She said the Umbra was returning, thickening in vacant buildings in the Northwest, which she called Nerland, a name I'd seen in the graffiti around town. Someone had painted the words on one of the overpasses: "Welcome to Nerland."

"What's the Umbra?"

"It's a spiritual force," she said. "Sister of darkness, mother of night."

"An older night than the night of the sun," Maya said.

The masks on the TV screen came in all sizes, shapes, and colors; some had horns and other protuberances. One man stood out in the crowd, a tall skinhead shaking a metal tube that made a hissing sound. His wiry frame was shudderingly tense, and his taut thin stomach swiveled in all directions as he gyrated before the camera. He wore a sleeveless leather vest, and his mask was sulphur yellow.

"In the demonic Umbra," Deirdre said, "the world will start to change. Everything will be affected. Government, big business, the lies. The country will implode."

Maya smiled dreamily.

The camera jerked into another room from which the sound of chanting emerged. The quality was excellent, not the least grainy. I saw a ring of masked skinheads and their females dancing like apes or lurching in place with candles shining in their hands as they hollered back and forth. When the cameraman panned to the couples in their midst I recognized Maya, her face blank as the moon. She was one of the white naked bodies writhing on a mattress. The lovers reached their collective climax as the tall skinhead exulted before them, shaking his ugly scepter. The video ended abruptly, without credits. It left me no more ill at ease than if I'd been hanging out with a bunch of film students.

Deirdre broke into wild laughter.

"You know that church on Vaughan Street?" she said. "The pretty one with the cupola? Well, ever since they closed it down it's become a magical place. We go in there a lot. The demons love us."

"I heard they were going to turn it into a dance club," Rex said.

"That would be cool. The Umbra in there is dark. You have the feeling it could do anything it wanted."

I stretched out on the rug as my head drifted pleasantly among a few light clouds. It was warmer inside the house than out. Maya let me fondle her great big breasts. Then Deirdre joined us with a kiss and sent Maya away.

"We're witches," Deirdre said. "Maya is my initiate. She is affirming her truth–her place in the universe. She is unlearning the lies of her childhood. Learning to see, to rupture the veil of cascading time."

Rex and I smiled. When we saw it wasn't the appropriate response, we stifled our laughter, glanced at each other, and laughed twice as loud. I thought back to freshman orientation, discussing rude male behavior with rich girls from the valley. But just from the newspaper I knew there were witches in the area. The Northwest has a lot of strange religious activity. Cults and covens. Some very nice people had told me stories about their past lives. They even revealed to me their real names, which they use in private. But this was my first encounter with witches.

I considered asking to see their witch certificates.

"Are there any men in your religion?" I said.

"Yes. Powerful head dancers, warlocks and watchers."

"Who's in charge, the men or the women?" Rex said bluntly.

She smiled and took up her earlier theme.

"The Umbra has a red gate tonight. We want to unlock it."

"What do you mean, a red gate?"

"It has to do with how the moon is poised."

"With how the moon is poised?"

"You have to get past the guardian. And to do that you have to get past yourself. The self you don't need. The self that society imposes on you. You have to exorcise the mask. Then you can use the magic. *Zine oben nustra.*"

Deirdre handed us a pair of masks that covered our faces. Then we followed her up a crooked staircase to a dark hall where I could scarcely see where I was going. In the hall she opened a door to a narrower and steeper flight of steps.

The narrow attic flickered with candle-light. There was only one window covered by a Venetian blind and flanked by posters: on one side the Twin Towers engulfed in fire and ruin, on the other the musician Oedipus Leech, masked and naked, his body covered with tattoos like continents on a map. The candle-flames, which trembled when we entered, straightened themselves in the darkness.

They burned in rows like sentinels on a wooden altar table, beyond which hung a glimmering partition of aluminum branches that toppled from a crossbeam. The tree must have been insane to the root: its foliage and fruit were shaped from the ugly husks of mass-produced beverages. Behind us loomed a grotesque sculpture, a breasted man with wings, fashioned entirely out of scrap metal. It glowered as we came in. Kneeling on a futon in a Chinese bathrobe Maya ignored us. She sat back on her heels, facing the altar with her hands resting above her knees. She was wearing a mask.

My head was an island of wine and weed as Deirdre fitted a golden mask over her eyes.

"Maya, do you open yourself to the Umbra?"

"Yes."

"Then light the first candle of Sheboth."

The girl rose, put an altar match to a tall candle on a crude metal stand, and turned sedately around. She removed her robe, which rustled to her ankles, and her naked body made a silhouette against the altar table. She dropped the mask behind her, baby-like, a torn reflection. Then she resumed her kneeling posture. Deirdre took a scissors and glided beside her on the futon. She pointed as she lifted the girl's dark hair, revealing a tattoo on her pale neck.

"This means she serves the chant. She is a chantress."

She brandished the scissors, which caught the light of the candles. Then she blew softly on the girl's neck where the black tattoo appeared, a flame in a diamond.

"The mark of the hierarchy," she said, clipping a strand of hair.

Rex and I watched in fascination as she touched the hair to the flame her initiate had lit, and dropped it burning in the shadow. When the faint acrid smell reached my nostrils I looked sideways at my brother, concealed behind a purple goblin face. A ghostly alarm was jangling my nerves.

"One of you say the chant with me, while the other removes his mask with Maya."

"And does what?" Rex asked, his voice edged with sarcasm.

"Sex," Deirdre said, meeting his thrust with imperious candor, "must be directed to certain ends."

The room was thick with smells.

"But we don't understand you at all," Rex said.

"You need to learn then," she said. "Say the chant."

"Why don't you say it by yourself?" he insisted.

"Say it with me," came her reply, soft and gentle. "Then it will be Maya's turn to chant..."

Taking a candle from the altar she began her chant, a litany of gibberish, calling the spirits to come, summoning the Umbra. Her voice welled out of her with freakish conviction. It rose like a flood around the naked girl. Then she cried more loudly and I could see the stud in her prolific tongue. Rex stood motionless. I had never seen him bend his will to anyone. Spells and enchantments glanced harmlessly off his psychic armor.

"You need to say the chant. It's the key to the gate."

Vaguely aware of being trapped, my thoughts staggered to the floor of my mind, like they were being isolated and weighed down. She had fed her fanatical vision until others tasted its force. In her way she was magnificent. I couldn't help admiring her.

"Come," Deirdre urged with a supple voice. "It's really very easy. You need to say the chant."

"Let's just have...have a nice time," I stammered, and a demon knocked at my ear and snickered at my lack of self-possession.

"Let go," she said softly, smiling. "Don't be repressed. Maya is a magical lover."

Still we hesitated. The candles flickered in their wax pools. The red and white flames sent shadows rippling through the crazy branches and garbage overhead.

"Say the chant and exorcise the mask."

Deirdre beckoned to me with her hand.

"Say the chant and exorcise the mask."

"Fuck the chant!" Rex shouted, unmasking himself.

She frowned. I felt the demons ranged like razors, ready to cut. But the spell was broken. We trampled down the stairs in the dark, grabbed our shirts, and pushed our way out. The streetlamps no longer illuminated the street but emitted a ghastly useless orange. Hurrying away I had a distinct sense of being watched, of a malevolent force pulsing on the back of my neck. A curtain fell in the silence, and I caught a glimpse of the old man with the dog, turning from the window of his house.

In preparation for LA, Rex and The Brains committed to a daily rehearsal schedule. We discovered that by staying sober and sticking
to a routine we could get things done. We concentrated on fourteen
songs with a couple of outsiders in case Luke Pound liked them.
Experimenting with arrangements and settling on the best versions
took all our spare time. We made constant use of the tape recorder.
Rex perfected his vocals and built up his parts as Hank and I figured out the right combinations of bass and drum.

That spring I saw the Grudas when we were setting up to play
at Kilroy's, or sometimes I just dropped in to say hello. Jack Gruda
and I became friends. He was a late, possibly unexpected addition
to the Gruda family, and our friendship gave him a sibling, just as
it gave me a surrogate mom and pop. Memorial Day was a week
away when he called me on the phone. A UPS truck had jumped
the guard-rail near the Morrison Bridge and hit his older brother
during rush hour. He bled to death on the interstate. Jack sounded
terrible. He'd never seen his father cry.

Saint Mary's Cathedral of the Immaculate Conception is in NW
Portland, a short walk from Kilroy's Tavern. It is a Byzantine struc-
ture of red brick. There is a marble baptismal font opposite the altar
when you come in, stained glass windows high in the nave, murals
on the walls of the apse, and lambent globes hanging from the cof-
fered ceiling. On entering the church I was met by a young woman
dressed in mourning black. She had been talking to an elderly couple who teetered off as the glass door of the alcove closed behind
me. Her manner was frank and welcoming.

"You're Jack's friend," she said, extending her hand. "I'm Sheila
Corcoran. Jack and I go way back."

Her face was quite beautiful, with almond-shaped eyes of
brown, a tall forehead, a Greek nose, and generous red lips. She
wore her hair up; it was thick rich auburn. Her complexion was fair.
She wore pearl earrings worked in silver.

Mourners were filling the cathedral. A middle-aged man in a
suit gave a weary wave as he passed by.

"Hi Dad," she said.

A woman started singing in a high sad voice. As she sang the
atmosphere of the church changed, like a faint wind rustling the
surface of a pool, the air becoming palpable. Not only the sound,

but the emotion resonated in the spacious contours of the wide interior.

"Would you like to sit with me?" Sheila asked in a polite, kindly way. "You can just pick a seat."

I slid into one of the pews as she genuflected in the aisle. Then she pulled down the kneeler from the back of the pew in front, and knelt praying with her hands together and her fingers intertwined. In a little while everyone rose. I could see Jack, his parents, and their family entering the cathedral from the front door. They went very slowly. Behind them came a flag-draped casket, trundling on a bier.

Like a marionette I followed the ritual of standing, sitting, and kneeling. The responses left me cold. After the Mass we tarried on the steps while Jack and the other pall bearers did their work. I saw Mr. Gruda, teary-eyed, talking with the priest beside the Cadillac hearse. The priest enfolded Mr. Gruda's hand between his own. Mrs. Gruda looked grim and determined, like she'd taken something to freeze her face. She was holding her grandson's hand. A little boy in black. The ceremony at the grave was surprisingly brief. The priest said a final blessing and they put the dead man in the ground.

Over lunch we started boozing it up. I tried the buffet and joined in conversation with Jack and Sheila. The funeral created a rapport between her and me that might not have happened otherwise. Jack was slapping me pretty hard on the back, getting a little reckless. At last I said goodbye and walked back to the cathedral to retrieve my car. When I turned off the engine I could hear Rex and Hank hard at work.

The first person we met in LA was a chauffeur with a seamy forehead. He was holding a handwritten sign that said "Fontay." It was our guy. The pallor of his countenance was like the ashes of hippiedom, offset by an unconquerable nose that was scarlet with drink. There burned the last flicker of a flame that blazed so brightly that summer, when the goddess of love tripped in the garden of youth, and in her wake there bloomed the rose, the lotos, and the starry asphodel. How changed! He had long gray hair that hung in a greasy curtain from the circumference of his bald spot. He wore a tight-fitting black suit like a mortician, and a white dress shirt that opened at the collar over a dirty white undershirt. Hauling our gear he limped like a three-legged horse.

His name was Buddy Young and we found him in the middle of a monologue. Once upon a time he used to play the clubs himself. He'd made a record that sold 100,000 copies. It was called *Forever Young*. Had we heard of it? No. Had he heard of us? No. Did anyone give a shit? No. He'd been through the whole circus, kids, house, divorce, child-support. Things had fallen to pieces.

"Fuck 'em if they can't take a joke," Buddy Young said, flipping the bird at the ceiling with a half-cocked gesture so that it pointed at the back of his head.

As we waited in the limousine he spat disdainfully out the window and fumbled around with a pile of papers on his lap. He said "shit" on a regular basis, like Old Faithful. He passed a few remarks about the President, who he said was a degenerate Nazi who came from a family of pigs. But they were smart.

"Don't get me started on the Bushes," he scowled, looking over his shoulder.

The country was a fascist state, only the Jews were in on it this time. It was the Jews and the Nazis. The Secretary of Defense was a fucking Nazi Jew. Even that black guy. What's-his-face.

But Buddy Young was a fighter.

"Like Stalin," I proposed.

"Shit, what are you, a smart ass?" Buddy Young said, hawking a final lugey out the window.

It kissed the ground with a smack.

He pressed a button and up rolled a glass divider between him and us. Then he played Led Zeppelin, which mingled with the palm trees and the tinted daylight until I somehow remembered a scene from *Jurassic Park*. The leather seat was cool and comfortable. I was fantasizing about Laura Dern as we coasted down the freeway and onto the crowded boulevards. Zepp was playing the immortal "Stairway to Heaven," a musical catastrophe without parallel, shudderingly horrible as a raptor disemboweling a retarded child, but you have to love that big guitar solo at the end. Laura. Gazing out the window Rex was coming home.

When we arrived Buddy Young rolled down the divider and presented his business card.

"Call me if you need anything," he said, laying on the charm. "Girls, boys, blow, you name it. Call me if you need a real guitar player."

Then he got out and opened the door for us. As he fetched our instruments Hank turned to me with a look of anguish. I'd never seen him so red in the face.

"Fucking jerk," he said.

"Geez, dude. What's wrong?"

"I'm Jewish."

A fact I'd forgotten.

"The guy's just a loser. It doesn't matter what he thinks."

"That's what they said about Hitler."

Randy Pace, Vice President of Crocodile Records, was waiting in the studio. I placed him as the man who'd seen us playing in Corvallis, when I awoke on a stranger's lawn. Wide, tall, and loose of limb, he possessed a jutting jaw, flaring nostrils, and heavy bags under his eyes. He wore a white sports coat and pinkish trousers. The three of us sat before the massive console and listened to Randy Pace. He had come to see us once more in the flesh. He loved the music and though it was unfortunately a business he wanted us to see him as a friend. He got kind of teary about it. His business was to make us part of the story of people who were stars and stars who were people.

"We're all just people," he concluded, cracking his knuckles as Buddy Young clopped in dragging the last of the gear like scrap metal.

An unshaven slob wearing a Ramones T-shirt entered from the side door in a cloud of cigarette smoke. Randy Pace introduced us to Keith Richter's old acquaintance, Luke Pound. We were impressed by Pound. He produced gold records. His talents were in demand. He collapsed in his armchair with a loud sigh and assessed his surroundings with self-pitying alertness.

"Fuck me," he said, dropping his lighter.

Then he told us he loved "Painkiller." He wanted to keep the rest of the album up to that level. He looked each of us in the eye and said there would be no drugs in the recording studio. We could all OD *after* the record was made, so far as he was concerned.

When we started working the truth struck home that Rex was

the main reason they signed the band. He had a great voice, handled his instrument professionally, and looked like a leading man. My stature improved when Luke Pound learned I wrote the lyrics. Thanks to rap, lyrics were getting more attention. The most pressure fell on Hank. Drums are quintessential and a producer has no end of options. In consequence most novices find themselves demoted to tambourine or cowbell. Not Hank, though. Like a young Joe DiMaggio he gave notice he could handle whatever you threw at him. It was a pleasure watching him hit the ball, which is a fine turn of phrase, so fuck off. And when he was established behind the drums, with the threat of studio players removed, he had a sunny disposition.

The intense busy days in the studio consumed even our fresh supplies of energy. Up at eight and over to Burbank, recording for twelve or fourteen hours, then back in bed by one or two. On the other side of the glass Luke Pound stopped us countless times, at the start of songs, in the middle eight, astride the final chorus. We could hear the mistakes, concentrated as we were with the cans attached to ears. We just didn't always agree they were important. One day Hank out of revenge stole our producer's cigarettes and he couldn't work the board because his fingers started shaking. It was then he confessed to being a recovering alcoholic. He'd spent the greater part of a decade in a state between drunkenness and a walking coma. He referred to it as "the scotch time." Another day he vanished from the studio for several hours only to reappear clean-shaven in a tuxedo. His third wife had just married his second wife's stepson. Luke Pound had given the bride away.

Penelope and Ellen weren't exactly on speaking terms. Ellen's zealous devotion to "that sad relic of patriarchy," in other words her family, put mother and daughter on opposite sides of a cultural battle line. Not that Penelope objected to families, per se, though she thought them archaic and preferred the term "extended relationships." It was her daughter's decision to stay home with her children that riled the author of *Women and Chaos*.

Ellen's husband, Emmanuel Mantica, had been in this country since high school. His father had fled the Sandinistas, whom he reviled. He departed his law practice one afternoon, boarded a plane with his wife and their five children, and landed in California. It was no easy thing, supporting them with a tire dealership in East LA. He made it the hard way in America. At the wedding Penelope clashed with Manny's father. Penelope called Fidel Castro a hero. Señor Mantica responded by swearing more and more violently in Spanish. The ensuing explosion probably could have been avoided had Penelope realized the old man wasn't agreeing with her.

When I visited San Bernardino the world seemed to be conspiring in a humorous prank. I was met at the door by three children, a four-year-old girl, a three-year-old boy, and a two-year-old girl, to whom I was known as Uncle Freddie. Call me a cubist, but I will forgo the quotation marks in an effort to include their perspective. They took me in without a moment's hesitation. They showed me their toys and books and the pages they colored. Carmen, the oldest girl, gave me a card she made herself, a heart with my name in it, also without quotation marks.

Ellen served potato soup, salad, and a roast. When the six of us gathered around the table, Julia, the baby, refused the high chair. In front of her Uncle she wanted to be like the big kids. Manny started the conversation by saying the music business had always interested him. His questions about the band were all good. How were the songs coming along? Did the producer understand our music? Where did we see ourselves in a year?

After supper, while Ellen attended to the kids, my brother-in-law invited me outside for a brandy. He dusted off the snifters and we retired to the deck.

"These are the long June days," he said, pushing back the chair to give his legs room.

I admired his wavy black hair and handsome features, but for a politician his accent seemed fairly thick. He swirled the brandy in his glass, put it down, undid a button on his shirt. Then he tapped two fingers on the table and passed a remark about politics. I wished I had something to say on the subject. Everyone I knew assumed politics to be absurd, unless it was radical politics. I didn't consider myself at all political. Fishing around for a comment I remembered there'd been a ruckus up in Oregon about the state budget. There was no money left for pensions. People were mad at the government. I looked at it, "government," like a big fat tuna hauled from the bowels of the sea. It gasped for air. It lay on its side and twitched.

"People fail to distinguish politics from economics. The government is a political institution. It has to be careful about its economic prerogatives. There are things that fall outside its natural scope."

The tuna caught my eye. It seemed to be blaming me, as if it was a victim of my own inexplicable violence. It looked wistfully at the sky, found nothing it liked, and went stiff. I felt kind of guilty.

"What about institutionalized racism?"

It was the magical phrase that saved my GPA in college. All you had to do to earn a "B" was to mention "institutionalized racism." The idea is that institutionalized racism is the worst kind of racism because it is invisible. It's like a virus and white males are the carriers. I grew fond of pointing out how "this very essay" was an example of institutionalized racism. It worked like a charm except the one time I took a leap and extended the argument to my handwriting. The professor, a black guy, obviously new, very inexperienced, wrote "How so?" in the margin. It shook my faith in creativity.

"Which institutions?"

"All of them," I said doubtfully. "Our whole society is racist."

"Says who?"

"My professors. It was practically the core of the curriculum."

"You went to Stanford, right? Well this might sound shocking to you. As a lawyer I can tell you the race industry is a big class-action law suit. In other words it's a shakedown and there's a lot of money at stake. Now here's the strategy. The carrot is calling whitey compassionate, which makes him feel good. The stick is calling whitey racist, which makes him feel bad. Independent blacks are Uncle Toms. Hispanics who think for themselves are traitors to their own people. If your opponent disagrees with you, he isn't just expressing an opinion, he's a hateful racist bigot. Freddie, are you a hateful racist bigot?"

"So you think there's no compassion involved?"

"There's more water on Mars. It was Nietzsche, you know, who talked about compassion as a mask for the will-to-power."

I am named after Nietzsche.

But Ellen interrupted our little dialogue. Manny had to say goodnight to the children and get to work. As we shook hands I studied his face with curiosity. He was a new type of animal to me. Thus I had to...

Thus?

She looked good, my sister. She wore her hair short and neat. The muscles in her arms and legs were nicely toned, I suppose from swinging all those kids around.

"The blessed hour when the children are in bed," she said, taking Manny's seat.

I asked her if she would ever go back to the law, and she surprised me by saying yes, when the kids were grown. She would be in her forties.

"Forty? It seems old."

"Oh, you'll change your mind."

The sprinklers came on and a bird started chattering on the roof. I sipped my brandy. The cloudless sky was expanding from blue to purple.

"Do you have a girlfriend?"

"Well, there's a girl I just met."

"Her name?"

"Sheila."

"That's an old-fashioned name."

"She's an old-fashioned girl. She goes to church."

Ellen said nothing, so we sat in silence awhile as the bird explored its range.

"Your husband's intense."

"My whole family."

She and I used to go ice skating in Palo Alto. We would bike over to the university in the sixty degree weather with our skates dangling from the handlebars. I used to miss the snowy winters back east. Ice skating lent substance to December in California.

"Why don't you and Penelope talk?"

Ellen put down her glass and folded her hands in her lap. Then she looked at the table.

"Sorry," I said. "We don't have to discuss it."

"No, it's all right. I want you to know. It's because of something that happened when I was in college."

"What happened, Ellen?"

She rose and turned the deck lights on. Then she poured a little bit of brandy into her wine glass and tasted it. Her voice was suddenly thick with emotion.

"I had an abortion when I was twenty. My first experience of intercourse and it made me pregnant. The guy of course urged me to have an abortion. It was so easy and cheap. You know, like in Hemingway, 'Just a little pinch, Jig, to let the air in.' I talked it over with...our parents. It seems like the only thing they ever agreed on in my life: my abortion. So I went through with it."

"Did it go okay?"

"I'm afraid so."

"Ellen, I just don't understand. You have to explain it to me. Did Penelope say something that hurt you?"

"Maybe you have to be the mother of small children..."

"Oh," I said; it was starting to register, like a faint pressure in my throat. "You feel like you've done something, uh, wrong."

"I murdered my baby," she said, as the tears flooded her eyes.

"It's all right, Ellen. You didn't know. How could you have known? I mean, how could you know what you'd feel later on?"

"Penny says I'm being ridiculous. She says I'm manufacturing feelings to fit my agenda. I hate that word, 'agenda.'"

"It's a lousy word."

She stood up and walked behind me and kissed me on the top of the head.

"Oh, Freddie," she said, like she was rocking a baby to sleep. "Little Freddie."

The next morning I poured myself a cup of coffee, took out my notebook, and sat down in the studio parking lot. I'd been dissatisfied with one of the lyrics. Now I rewrote it in a few hours. It was called "Jig."

> *VERSE*
> *I knocked a whore up*
> *Her only name was Jig*
> *Three months later she was*
> *high at every gig*
> *We went back to her room*

Her beauty was appealing
She didn't seem to know me
as she stared up at the ceiling
CHORUS
Throw it into stainless steel
Tell yourself it isn't real
Tender tender tender veal
VERSE
They love her at the clinic
She never has to pay
Finishes by five o'clock
and feels a little gray
I'm always glad to see her
She knows my every whim
She's creamy smooth as butter
but she spreads herself thin
REPEAT CHORUS
VERSE
She whispers to her son
when nobody is there
He's not a real person
He's just a pinch of air
She lies awake and stares at him
His beauty is angelic
and when she summons him by name
it's fucking psychedelic
REPEAT CHORUS

I liked it better than what we had on tape and Rex agreed to re-do his vocals. Luke Pound mixed the song with a fade-out of Rex shouting the word "tender," making it loop around over and over again.

FOUR
The Princess and the Dragon

When Penelope flew in for the Fourth of July we hadn't seen her in a while. She'd been lecturing at Stanford and at conferences from Reykjavik to Cape Town. She planned to be in town for three days. Then it was off to Rotterdam and Munich, or Zurich, I forget.

During a free moment she'd mailed us a glossy photograph of Hiroshima after the blast, suggesting we make use of it. Crocodile liked the idea. The artist superimposed a shot of the band playing live onto a demolished bridge in front of a skeletal dome. It looked totally real.

I showed the newly minted CD to Mr. Gruda over at Kilroy's. He studied the artwork.

"What does it mean, Freddie?" he asked.

"I don't know, Mr. Gruda. I don't know what it means to tell you the truth."

"People who complain about Hiroshima have no idea what the hell that war was like. Our POWs were dying like flies. The Japs killed our boys for sport."

His anger slowly broke through the stony demeanor behind which he had lately resigned the world. His lower lip trembled, as his thoughts gathered and arranged themselves.

"People say there were signs the Japs would surrender. That's bull. People say FDR knew about Pearl Harbor. It's all bull. The Japs would have dug in just the way they did at Okinawa. There is no tougher defender than the Jap. How many died at Hiroshima? Eighty thousand? The Invasion of Japan would have cost ten Hiroshimas. On our side alone. You can write that down. It's a goddamn fact."

Rex was playing solo for a college radio station, so I agreed to meet Penelope and her boyfriend, Adrian Larrouturou, at PDX. Before turning forty Adrian had concluded a volatile and kinky love affair with the wife of a French politician. Her detailed account of the relationship achieved a *succès de scandal* in the French press. Happily for Adrian the scandal brought with it a series of job offers. His career, which was stalled, roared into the fast lane. Then it skipped over the Atlantic. Recently he'd taken up residence with Penelope. I can't say that he has ever published anything of significance. But if old habits prevail, he is at work this very day on a dense manuscript called *Une vie théorique*.

Adrian emerged first from the plane, elegantly dressed in a glossy silver suit with a youthful cut. He was tall and devoutly thin. His sleek head was bald and white. She was wearing a sky-blue blouse of fine silk, a short lilac skirt, and elegant sandals. She appeared to have been starving herself. I think they were quarreling. They said nothing to each other even as they exchanged friendly greetings with me. Outside in the sunlight I noticed the lenses of Penelope's glasses were changing from a soft gray to an impenetrable violet. He seemed to notice this too since he stopped dead in his tracks and pulled out his shades with a flourish. I stood by as they tested the wind with their delicate noses like a pair of visiting dignitaries.

The three of us went out for lunch at Jake's. They were glad the term was behind them and over cocktails they warmed to each other's company. Adrian described how the commencement speaker, a cabinet member from the Reagan administration, was knocked unconscious during a speech on the fall of the Berlin Wall. There was a fine mist and then a terrible crackling noise as the speaker's lip froze to the microphone and he started to convulse.

"The poor bastard," Penelope said, sipping her Manhattan. "We were cheering as they rolled in the gurney."

"The fascists!" Adrian said, shaking his fist. "Let them try to shit in France. We will show them."

The waiter came by with another round of drinks. He left with the information that the lobster bisque was a bit thin.

"You know who Bush's favorite philosopher is?" Adrian asked, beginning to smile.

Penelope was laughing now too.

"Jesus Christ! His favorite philosopher is Jesus Christ! Moses is second. Moses and the burning Bush."

I mentioned that *Painkiller* had gotten a rave review in the LA Musical World. This drew Adrian's full attention.

"I'm a little uncertain about rock," he confessed. "It seems to be losing its–how do you say?–its *itch*."

"Its *edge*," Penelope corrected him.

He fired a vicious glance at her and turned calmly to hear my response. There was none.

"You don't believe in the little kingdom of man, do you?" he said, peering over his sunglasses as he asked me this bizarre question. "Look at it from the point of view of the minute one-eyed co-pepod," he seemed to suggest.

"Adrian adores *Painkiller*," Penelope said, clearing her throat. "But he has no faith in popular culture. He says that virtually nothing, not even the most sophisticated art, can escape the alienation of life in late capitalist society."

"How do you see it?"

"I'm afraid there will be nothing left in a hundred years," she sighed. "Unless we can get the idiots who run this country to start reading Fanon and Foucault."

"But there are no flying pigs," Adrian remarked, draining his vodka gimlet.

The release party for *Painkiller* took place at the Pyramid Club, on Front Avenue in NW Portland near the Fremont Bridge. The new club occupied a former warehouse, fashionably renovated by a portly young fellow named Bill Barnes, whose family helped settle Portland when Rutherford B. Hayes was in the White House. Bill Barnes had taken a large sum of old money, invested it in some silly dot coms, and dumped his enormously overvalued stock the day before the bubble burst. He was always smiling. How Bill Barnes met Ed Smith I don't know. They spent money lavishly on the new club, rearranging the huge space and outfitting it with a stage, a dance floor, Egyptian moldings, marble rest rooms, hieroglyphic engravings, a plaster-of-paris mummy in its own stately sarcophagus, and a golden scarab for every door. So that's where your investment went.

It started out a fun night. Penelope and Adrian treated us to a spendy dinner; I had the duck and washed it down with an excellent French wine. Then we drove to our reserved parking space at the club. On the sidewalk a searchlight proclaimed the event to the heavens, prodding a caravan of clouds with its imperious beam. But the clouds were sluggish beasts, and kept to their own pace, indifferent to the little lights below. A magazine writer intercepted us at the door and Adrian started pontificating. As soon as he deployed the term "culture industry" I slipped behind it and pushed my way forward.

In the dressing room I discovered a cache of champagne–Randy Pace wished us good luck. Mrs. Cove sent a bouquet. Her son was a busy man at that hour, tuning guitars, twiddling knobs and buttons, testing his equipment for the mass of bodies in the room. Ed Smith came in, draped a skinny arm around me, and reintroduced Bill Barnes, who thought everything I said was hilarious. I said I liked his tie and he laughed. I told him I was nervous and he laughed. I told him Ed had no sense of humor and they erupted with furious laughter. As Rex, Hank, Penelope, and Adrian emerged Ed poured champagne into a ring of long-stemmed flute glasses.

"It is a little known fact..." Bill Barnes began, pinching the stem of his glass.

"I don't believe in facts!" a French accent declared to general laughter.

"To *Painkiller*!" Ed Smith exclaimed.

"To *Painkiller*!"

"May you never sell out," Bill Barnes said.

"Not on your life," John Beazler said, sweeping into the room and usurping Rex's upraised glass. "Thank you, my boy. If you're going to sell out, for God's sake don't let me know."

He quaffed the champagne in a single gulp and graciously returned the empty glass. Then he faced Bill Barnes, making a Puff Daddy move with his hands. The proprietor squinted in vain to interpret him.

"Violence is not the answer," Beazler said.

From the stage I could see only gray smoky air and the blurred outlines of the crowd. Checking my instrument I glanced up and noticed Rex standing beside me.

"What a nut house," he said.

I said, "Remember when we saw The Rolling Stones?"

"Yeah, we were twelve."

"What did Mick say to the crowd?"

He returned to his microphone with a grin.

"Would somebody please take her clothes off," he said.

Hank tapped out the four count for "Wire Monkey," the first song from the album. We had every inch of the routine down. The lights flashed like gunpowder as the first chord ripped the air. Even the crowd knew what to do. In about two seconds I wasn't nervous at all. I caught Weez's eye and he gave me a big thumbs up.

Ten minutes later Rex was changing his guitar and soliloquizing into the microphone. He was developing a rivalry with Van Sligo, the famous Irish rock star.

"...I turn on my cable and there he is, back from another seven-course dinner. I think he'd had the duck. He was riding through the fields of Ireland. The beautiful Irish fields. It was snowing and things were in their glory..."

A girl who'd been dancing just below me, one of the ones we called "priestesses" for their flowing dresses like tapestries and whirling hands above their heads, tapped me on the boot. As I knelt down I noticed she might be forty, maybe more.

"You and your brother look like movie stars," she said. "You're gorgeous."

"Van Sligo and David Bowie are making an album," Rex pattered on. "It's called Ziggy Stardust and the Billionaire from Dublin."

"Thanks," I nodded courteously and started to pull away; but her hand clung to my boot.

"I'm Darla," she said, like she was announcing one of the seven mysteries.

Then she kissed the tip of my damn boot.

Christ, I thought, she's my mother's age. As we began another song, I surveyed the dance floor and noticed Penelope and Adrian. They were boogying away, having a ball of a time.

But Jack and Sheila were no shows, despite my having placed their names on the guest list. It was the last set and I'd given up on them when I saw Jack dancing drunkenly alone. Glass precariously in hand he was doing little cha-cha steps in a corner. Then he tried to cha-cha with a girl, whose boyfriend took umbrage and pushed him so that he spilled his drink. Jack set his glass down, cha-cha'd back over, and coldcocked the poor sap with a single punch. It happened during a break-down where the bass riffs by itself: I was doing it for the thousandth time, no need to think about it, as I watched the man's body sway like timber. The bass drum started to beat just as his head bounced off the floor.

I hurried over to Jack, who was making an ass of himself lying on his back.

"Is the guy okay? D'ya think?"

The guy didn't look too good.

I said, "Looks like he'll be fine."

"So you've met Mister Congeniality," Sheila said, suddenly appearing.

"Sorry," Jack mumbled.

When the police arrived they escorted the guy to the hospital and Jack to the slammer. He kept mumbling "sorry" to everybody within earshot, me, Sheila, Ed Smith, Bill Barnes, the girl whose friend he clobbered, the cop who cuffed him.

Sheila said she needed to look after Jack. So after we finished the set I found myself by her side in the lobby of the city jail. It was a sterile, harshly lit room where drunks, addicts, hookers, thieves, and other superstars shuffled in and out among the bleary-eyed police who vetted them. Sometimes I hallucinate a little and imagine the life span of a stranger trailing in afterimages behind him. But the kids being brought in, young teenagers working the street– I knew they would never grow old. For a while a social worker named Burton argued back and forth with the cops. I don't know how it ended. We caught a break because Sheila recognized one of the officers, who relayed the important news that the guy Jack punched was fine and declined to press charges.

The telephone was ringing as I woke from an interminable sound-check. It was Mrs. Gruda. I glanced over at the bed where her impeccable son lay sleeping it off. I said he was out buying bread.

The boy soon stirred. He rose ash-white and naked, wished me good morning in a raspy voice, and made a beeline for the bathroom. He was in there for a good fifteen minutes, dispensing nectar. I rubbed my stiff neck and stared at the wall, where a galaxy of motes revolved in a sunbeam. He ran the shower and returned looking like himself.

"What is it with you two?" I asked, as we organized our breakfast of Apple Jacks, toast, and instant coffee.

"She's an old friend," he said, chortling to himself. It wasn't a happy sound.

"Did you work with her?"

"No. She's a tour guide."

"A tour guide?"

"At Washington Park."

"Would you tell me what happened last night?"

"It's a long story."

"Indulge me."

He scraped off the burnt from a piece of toast, buttered what remained, and took a bite. I could still taste the duck.

"Last night? No, it was Wednesday, two nights ago. She and I drove down to Front Avenue. You know, to see the ships–no big deal. Then we had a drink and I said something stupid and she got angry. Don't look so surprised. In high school we used to joke about it–hooking up. But she's changed."

"What do you mean?"

"Something happened..."

I could tell he was disgusted with himself. Jack was never a bad guy, only a bit spoiled. As he rummaged through his desk he balled up several pieces of paper and tossed them into the trash before he found the letter he wanted and opened it.

"Where is it? Here it is. '...the fact that earthly beauty and love can be a portal to spiritual awakening and embodiment.' She spent a lot of time with a priest."

"That reminds me. Your mother called. Just before you woke up."

"Is she okay?"

"I think so."

He walked over to the window, opened it all the way, and farted.

"Lovely weather we're having."

"What happened last night was that I got to the Pyramid Club pretty late. I went straight to the bar and found myself staring at Sheila. So I knocked down a few more drinks and coasted onto the dance floor."

"You coasted, all right. Like Gregory Hines. But didn't you talk to her at the bar?"

"Not that I recall. She was sitting at the other end. Some guy was hitting on her. There's always some guy hitting on her."

"Well, she seems to care for you."

He put the letter back and hung his head.

"She's a good person, Freddie."

The next week I paid a visit to Washington Park. I was wandering through the Japanese Gardens, drinking in the chrysanthemums, when I saw Sheila in a green blazer leading a group of tourists. I hung around and when the tour finished she came over to say hello.

"I didn't know you liked gardens," she said.

"Don't tell anyone."

"Well, it's a beautiful day," she said.

"So far."

There were people everywhere, people playing tennis, posing for pictures, lolloping off to inspect aisles of roses, which seduced the eye with a gaudy display of dark reds, soft pinks, pulsating yellows and oranges, and hybrid combinations of splashing color. The grass was shining. As we fell into conversation and strolled down to the amphitheater, past the scent of these obstreperous roses, something struck me for the first time that I would never entirely forget in days to come, though I struggled by turns to suppress or to ignore it: I mean how men, young men and old men, gazed as she passed, their faces transparent with piteous longing.

I touched her for a few facts. She graduated from college the year after me. She was an only child. Her mother died when she was little.

"God, I'm sorry."

"That's okay."

"Was she ill a long time?"

"Brain aneurysm. It happened out of the blue."

"Do you remember her?"

"It's a long time ago. Now and then something returns–the other day it was the smell of her perfume. It was like she was in the room."

Her father was an architect. He was a devout Catholic.

"How devout?"

"He has a picture of himself and the Pope in his study."

In college she was a double major in music and theology. She was applying to graduate school. She didn't like "twelve-tone."

"I was wondering why you went out of your way for Jack the other night."

"Because I care for him," she said with simple gravity.

"But doesn't it seem like a game? Boy chases girl. Girl chases boy."

"Men and women hurt each other," she said gently. "If that's what you mean."

An orange frisbee came skidding to a halt at our feet. She picked it up and sent it sailing over the head of the thrower. He jumped like an elephant.

"Lousy throw!" he shouted.

We laughed and sat back down and smiled in the sunshine. From the amphitheater steps we could see no more of Portland than the tops of tall buildings bobbing up and down in the high leafy branches. Across the river the near hills were brown with patches of soft green, the far ones a hazy blue. Mount Hood planted its feet on the horizon like a friendly giant overseeing his domain.

"Have you eaten lunch?"

"Have I eaten lunch?" she echoed, scrutinizing my face.

"We could just walk down the hill. Get a sandwich or something."

"I have a car."

We settled on a delicatessen over by the baseball stadium, a popular eatery where we waited for a table. As we glanced at the menu Sheila asked about my family. She was interested in Ellen because Ellen was juggling motherhood and a career. Her interest seemed to grow when I thought to mention that Ellen and Manny were Catholic. I liked the sound of her voice and I had nothing else to say. An awkward silence followed. Then I asked about her green blazer.

"I'm going for a golf look," she deadpanned.

"Do you play?"

"What?"

"Golf."

"Never. It makes me think of TV. I really don't like TV. Do you?"

"I'd rather read...*TV Guide.*"

"What else do you read?"

"Nothing. I really don't read anything. I've never liked ink."

"Why are all the good-looking men jerks?"

I noticed that Sheila's face was active when she spoke, with big eyes and quick eyebrows, as if she was passing judgment not only on what she said but on how she said it. Then she would stare at me angelically.

We had just paid the check when Johnny D came strutting in like a young Paul McCartney. He was putting up posters for a show. He took us in stride.

"Either of you guys want one?" he asked, brandishing a poster with his handsome mug on it.

"No thank you," Sheila said, heading toward the exit.

I grinned back at him.

"Only if you sign it."

Sheila pushed the door open and kept going. After a few dumb words with Johnny, I left the restaurant and ran to catch up with her.

"Look," she said. "They're gutting it."

It was The Matterhorn. Its disassembled kitchen cluttered up the sidewalk where a moving company was loading equipment. As we hurried past Sheila regarded the scene without further comment. Could she have heard about Beazler's little operation? In the parking lot men were busy with booths and chairs and tables. She was quickening her pace.

"Listen," she said when we reached her car. "I'm afraid I've got to get back to work. Can I offer you a lift somewhere?"

"Why don't we hook up on Friday then," I suggested. "Not hook up. I mean just hang out. Get together."

"I don't think I can make it. But thanks anyway. It was nice to see you."

Baseball fans were pressing into the stadium behind us and as the light changed a little runt in socks and shorts ran into the street chasing a pack of older kids. He tripped on the tracks just as the shuttle started navigating the corner. I was the closest person so I hauled the kid up. I just swung him back to the sidewalk and set him on his feet. All the while the shuttle driver was pounding his horn. The little scamp gave me a sharp look and darted off like nothing.

Sheila gazed after the boy as he ran after his friends.

"I guess I'll see you later," I said.

"You don't have to perform Friday night?"

"No. Our tour starts the next day. So I have Friday off."

"Well...why not?" she said, smiling.

"Our car's busted. I'll have to meet you."

"That's fine."

"Alexis's at eight? Do you know it? The Greek restaurant on Burnside."

"I know where it is. I'll see you at eight."

Ed Smith was staying home. Bill Barnes invited him to run the Pyramid Club and there were questions about his contract with the band. Crocodile wanted to buy him out and he needed to review his options. We would have Weez along for support now that he had proved he could handle the board. Then Rex added another surprise by proposing that Beazler join us in the capacity of tour manager.

"He's smart, you know," Rex said. "He leads his own band, and they're good."

"I know he's smart. I also know he keeps you in drugs."

"Beazler is a force of nature."

"Fallen nature."

Hank joined the debate. He said he couldn't see my point of view. If Beazler got out of line we could sack him. The tour was only a few weeks anyway. So we voted and I lost. When I asked Weez what he thought of our new tour manager he shook his head in disgust. He conceded Beazler was smart, but he didn't trust him.

On a hot July day we held a major organizational meeting at the Pyramid Club. In attendance were the band, Beazler, Weez, and

Randy Pace, who was taking a special interest in us. Beazler began with the business of the itinerary. The *Painkiller* Tour would open Saturday night in Vancouver, BC, followed by Sunday night in Seattle, Monday in Spokane, Tuesday in Yakima, Wednesday in Tacoma, Thursday in Olympia, Friday in Corvallis, Saturday in Eugene, then down Route 101 to the Bald Eagle in Eureka. After that, a day off, followed by Tuesday in Sacramento, Wednesday in Berkeley, and Thursday and Friday in San Francisco. Then we had Saturday night off in Palo Alto because we were booked in the Palladium on Sunday. From there it was Tuesday in Santa Cruz, Wednesday in Monterey, Thursday in Santa Barbara, and on to LA.

Next Randy Pace gave a report. He was contacting college radio stations, getting airtime for *Painkiller*, and setting up appearances and interviews, which might be added on short notice. They bought advertising in several media and a poster would be sent to retailers by the end of next week. Randy Pace handed Beazler a folder of glossies of the group, a cell, and a green and brown briefcase displaying the company's Crocodile logo. As the loot piled up Beazler said he needed a laptop and some accounting software. The Crocodile man didn't blink.

"These boys are going to the top," Beazler said. "I want them to have the best."

"So do we," Randy Pace said, reaching into a gold shopping bag and revealing–presto!–a box of Trojans.

"What the hell?" Rex said.

I said, "I hope they're not the kind you have to pre-heat."

"One of our bands had to cancel halfway through a national tour because they all had the clap. By the time they got to Chicago nobody could pee. I had to fly in a doctor. Now I don't want that to happen to you boys. That's why I'm telling you these things. The safest form of sex is just a nice clean blow job."

"And you can leave the young woman a complimentary copy of *Leaves of Grass* if you're feeling sentimental. We could put a stack beside the condoms."

"That's right," he continued. "No fuss, no muss. And whatever you do, avoid underage women."

I said, "Avoid what?"

"Underage women."

"I don't understand. What exactly are you saying?"

"Don't fuck little girls."

"Well, thanks Mr. Pace," Beazler said diplomatically. "I would suggest that we say a prayer together."

Beazler bowed his mighty head. Randy Pace seemed ready to go with the idea.

"Say it, Reverend!" Rex shouted. "Hallelujah, brother!"

"Holy Father," Beazler intoned, "keep us from the celibate, from the clap, and all officers of the law. But send us the daughters of our enemies, and their wives also, but not their mothers. And lead us into temptation as quickly as you possibly can. Amen."

After dinner at Alexis's Restaurant Sheila and I crossed Burnside Street in the rain and walked over to the Chocolate Moose on the corner of Ankeny Street and Second Avenue. A crowd of twenty crammed the small cozy tavern with laughter and talk and smoke. We entered at just the right moment to claim the sole unoccupied booth.

As the waiter took away the last traces of the previous occupants, the topic of conversation turned to religion. I commented that Catholicism was old and obscure. You have to change with the times.

"I see you've learned your lesson," Sheila replied. "It's hard to say what's better about the media: its breadth or its depth."

She held up an imaginary microphone and spoke into it affecting the pompous accent of TV journalism.

"Protesters gathered this afternoon to challenge the Catholic view that human beings are superior to pigs. Animal rights activists splattered themselves with blood and called for an end to human reason. Parishioners we spoke to looked worried and the bishop did not return our call..."

"Very funny. You're not being preachy, are you?"

"Yes. I'm fond of my cannibal religion."

"What do you mean by that?"

"God becomes bread," she said, softening her voice.

"Transubstantiation."

Coincidentally, the waiter, who doubled as bartender, returned with a carafe of red wine and left it on the table with two glasses.

"Very good," Sheila said. "Any other questions?"

"Why do Catholics kneel in church? Doesn't it seem outdated?"

"Oh, like it's just God hanging out."

"Explain it to me then."

"If you like," she said, looking at her glass. "But I could use a sip of wine."

It took a moment but I realized it would not be entirely inappropriate for me to fill our glasses.

"Kneeling," I said, having successfully managed the wine.

"Okay," she said. "If you want to know, it feels right. I mean that's God on the cross. It might help to think of God as not being Freddie Fontane, or Sheila Corcoran, or whoever you like. I would never kneel to myself or my own..."

"...image? But don't you think the church betrays women? I mean they're on their knees before a man. It's like training."

"What does your sister think?"

"I'm asking you."

"I think it protects them."

Lord knows it is a pleasure watching a beautiful woman drink her wine. I cannot stand a girl who sips at her glass like a move in a three-hour chess game.

"Go ahead," I said, sensing she had more to say on the subject. "Enlighten me."

"You're saying the church is patriarchal. But maybe you need some patriarchy. After all, you know what matriarchy is..."

"I have a feeling you're going to tell me."

"The mothers are all that's left because the fathers take no responsibility. They just slip away and do their thing."

"Like musicians, you mean."

I noticed she was blushing over her wine. I know which was the prettier shade of red. A blush is such a delicate effect. You scarcely ever see people color anymore.

"I just realized something."

"What?"

"You're the first girl I've ever dated in my life."

"Is that what this is—a date?"

"Yes. I'm certain of it. This is a bona fide date."

"Well, how do you feel?"

"*Embarrassed.*"

"Really?"

She was wearing a cranberry blouse, a simple affair, but it was cut low enough to reveal God's own acre of creamy white cleavage.

"No. It's a lot like bowling. You know, you stare at the rack and aim for the pins."

"I think I see that bowling ball now," she said, shading her eyes and watching with an increasingly worried look. "A small dark object rolling towards eternity"–she gave a sharp wince–"in the gutter."

"Ah, but the game's not over."

"You'll need to work on your approach."

By the time we finished the wine it was late. I needed to hurry to catch the last bus. We were leaving the next day for Vancouver.

Outside the tavern the rain was steady. Voices from inside started singing. She opened her umbrella.

"Would you like me to kiss you? Or should we shake hands, Miss Corcoran? I do so enjoy a nice firm handshake."

Hobbling past a wet tramp fixed a sore, sour eye on me. He was twisted like a pretzel.

 "Bullshit," he said with conviction.

"I know a place where you can stay the night..."

I assumed an expression of total innocence.

"It's a rectory. Why don't you sleep there, and then we can go to Mass in the morning, before you go on tour?"

"Mass?"

"Yes, it would be good for you."

We drove to a three-story house in SE Portland. She had the key to the place. We entered quietly and she led me to a bare room with a cot. Scribbling a note for one of the priests she posted it on the door, arranged for my comfort, and said she'd see me in the morning.

A fist knocked heavily on the door at 7:15. When I opened it I saw an eighty-year-old man wearing a white robe with a cord around his waist. His eyes were blue stones. He was going to celebrate Mass in the chapel at 7:30.

"You had better move it," he said, walking away with Sheila's note in his hand.

I examined my unshaven face, splashed cold water on it, and hurried down the street. I found Sheila waiting for me. It was a small stone church, simple and intimate, with a plain sanctuary and an ivory crucifix. I suppose it must have had a name. There was a series of stained glass windows on the wall we sat by, and they struck me as peculiar. In the first place, their color glowed. The morning sun was facing the front and not the side of the church, but they shone as it were directly or from within. I think they were meant to tell a story. In one panel there was a lady in a blue robe, with mourners carrying her bier in front of a row of trees. In the next panel, the bier was empty and the mourners looked stunned. In the third panel, a boy was raising a lock of hair to the sky.

There is standing when the priest comes in. Then a part where you sit and somebody reads from the Big Book. Then the priest reads (you stand) and talks (you sit). Then you sing while you pay. Then there is standing followed by kneeling followed by standing and the Our Father. Then everybody shakes hands, a well-intended gesture no doubt but fraught with anxiety and clearly the weak spot of the ritual. Then the kneelers get pushed back up and there's shuffling of feet and they line up for the Ritz. Then the kneelers come back down for additional kneeling. Then a last brief spell of sitting and standing.

I made no sense of the liturgy, except the line "he suffered, died, and was buried." It reminded me of that famous dog named Lucky. You know, the one with the three legs. Halfway through I glanced at my watch and could have sworn it had stopped. Still, considering the effect of the whole, I could see how it appealed to certain demographics, like priests and nuns, people with unsteady memories, those who think a lot about dying, and widows or the like who want to pray for the dead.

Afterwards we joined Brother John in the refectory. Our long table matched the room: scrubbed and worn, clean and dry. The other priest wasn't around. We drank a pot of coffee and ate oranges and plain bagels, which are by far the best kind of bagel, a savory bread. The friar had the wrinkled pallor of advanced old age. His eyes were sore and red at the lids and his lips were thin and pale. I liked his wrinkles, though, deep grooves that scored his flesh like the plough of years. He sat before me, a wise and ancient ape.

"You do not think that you are going to save this scalawag?" he asked incredulously.

"He's not all that bad," Sheila said, laughing. "His band is going out on tour today."

"Very nice," he said. "A rock star. I suppose your idea of virility is to claim as many conquests as possible."

I blinked dumbly at this remark. Apparently the wise and ancient ape was cantankerous. Was he referring to my specific interest in Sheila or to my general interest in women? In either case the question didn't reflect well on me.

"The word 'cad' seems to have dropped out of the English language. Do you know what a cad is?"

"No," I said.

"A cad is a perversion of a gentleman."

"I've never met any gentlemen."

"In that case you might consider who your friends are."

My eyes visited Sheila. She regarded me sympathetically, almost maternally; but she was deferring to the friar.

"Sheila and I are friends."

"Really?" he inquired. "Do you think young women can afford to be friends with men whose idea of manhood is virtually canine?"

His unusual assumption was that I should be interested in what he had to say, and that he had some special office to perform in expressing himself.

I said, "I thought priests were supposed to be, well, tolerant of others."

"I have noticed in life," he said slowly, "those who are tolerant of everything have exceedingly low expectations."

Sheila looked more anxious now. But I wasn't angry. He wasn't talking to make a sale or win me over. He was clearly interested in protecting her. He was a very old man who cherished no illusions, except maybe one great big one. I found something admirable in his having spoken so forcibly. By nature I have always taken instruction surprisingly well. I have taken it and left it on the nearest trash heap.

"So what do you suggest?"

"I suggest that you learn to be a man. Recover your God-given dignity. It will be a painful experience."

I thanked him and pleaded the exigencies of time. I told him I would remember his words. He gave me a limp handshake and dismissed me with an air of disdain.

When we pulled into the driveway, just an hour before the tour bus was scheduled to depart from the Pyramid Club, Rex had already gone. Hank was out in the pasture talking with the caretaker. One of the calves was sick.

"What about Jack?" I asked her.

"He's joining the Army."

"His father was in the Army..."

She had something for me. A medal on a chain.

"Brother John wanted you to have this."

"Thanks...I liked him. My kind of friar."

"Be good, cowboy," she said.

I kissed her and took her hand unawares and squeezed it gently just before we parted. Then she drove off, up the gravel drive, onto the busy road.

FIVE
Sin

At first Beazler impressed me in his new role as tour manager. He kept Rex's habit under control, or at least it was out of sight. He refined his inscrutable manner, becoming more than a match for the club owners and their dingy surrogates, most of whom were seasoned swindlers eager to rip us off. He spent hours on his cell, coordinating our schedule with Randy Pace. The two of them established a rapport. Beazler was no longer just a drug dealer. He was a rising junior executive, a spry young devil with a future.

With Brother John's reprimand stinging my ears I sought after my God-given dignity for about forty-eight hours. *Painkiller* started selling surprisingly well, and temptation followed exactly like a good-looking drunken wench. Now the rule of the road is that the most desirable girl, the most deliciously bouncy and enticingly dressed, gets the star. The girls were competing for Rexy boy, and they could be pretty cutthroat about it. Mostly teenagers, and God knows maybe fifteen in some cases, they pinched and taunted and heckled each other. One time one of these hotties ripped off her top and waved it around the hotel suite like a rebel flag. So the other girls took their shirts off too, twisting and screaming in a pleasant rite for which Rex was the priest, or maybe the god, since they would have set innocence on fire to catch his eye and become one with him.

A few of the girls were older, college types who spoke a language I knew. I speak of my mother tongue, feminism, only a kind of sluttish dialect that said "let's fuck" like you were ordering a cheeseburger. These girls looked the raunchiest of all. In some lost hour I got into a slapping contest with a blonde from Evergreen and she got bossy and whacked me pretty hard. So I whacked her pretty hard in return. For some reason I pulled back from really just whacking the hell out of her, which, now that I reflect, should have been the natural result of our little crawl through the abyss. Blame it on my old-fashioned upbringing.

Weez and I went out several times for breakfast. At least I had breakfast. One night we noticed a Denny's just a block from our hotel. As usual I ordered the Grand Slam. Weez polished off a Reuben sandwich, french fries, and a milkshake. I took it for granted that he drank large chocolate milkshakes at 3:00 am. They seemed to help him sleep.

Near us were two crowded tables, each with half-a-dozen guys, the same age as ourselves. The one group slouched in their seats. Every head sported a baseball cap, worn uniformly backwards. To look closely at these young men was to realize they had signed no social contracts. Civilization, school, work, the future, were so many hypotheticals in an experiment that had only a faint purchase on their emotions. None of these fellows met your eye. Body and mind were hard and raw.

At the next table sat a ring of more sensitive-looking chaps, laughing and discussing contemporary music. They dressed stylishly. One of them pleaded his case against a band he disliked, and the others responded with a flurry of giggles. When they grew loud, a wounded voice cried out, "No, no, no!" Somehow they had a girl in their midst. She was a tanned brunette in a red tank top, with more chest than her companions. It looked like she had made a difficult and luckless choice between the two groups. She kept up a numb smile, like someone submitting to an ironical dentist.

What happened was that one of the barbarians scooped an angel fish out of the aquarium behind him. The fish departed its native element with hardly a struggle, hung by its dorsal fin in mid-air, and, arriving at the next table, dove summarily into a tall glass of diet Sprite. Did it float? Yes. Registering the change in its environment the paralyzed fish lay like a silver coin on the crushed and bubbling ice.

Now if the boys on the receiving end of this transaction were gay, it occurred to me I might be looking at a hate crime. And PETA might want my testimony also. There can't be anything ethical about dropping a tropical fish into a soft drink. Over at the salad bar a group of drag queens was wielding tongs and shedding a peculiar glamour. But even with heels and wigs and padding they flaunted a perverse masculinity, a comical swashbuckling edge, which the pretty boys lacked.

Note for a lyric:

> *We lost our balls*
> *In shopping malls*
> *Taking wireless telephone calls.*

The wimps glared collectively at the barbarians. One of the baseball caps started to guffaw, but the others corrected him–and not without effect. Their studied indifference created a feeling of random menace.

The barbarians had attacked the wimps at their most vulnerable point: right before their eggs got cold. Now there was no choice for the wimps but to combine frowning and eating, eating and frowning, in a mournful silence as if the salt on their omelets was jeering at them.

"Let's go save the fish," I said to Weez.

"It's long gone now," he replied. "...I'd hate to be that girl."

I said, "Explain yourself."

"She can't be happy," he explained.

"Yeah?"

"Come on, Freddie. She reminds me of my sisters. Those jerks are insulting her."

"Her? I thought they were insulting her boyfriends."

"I tell you she's at the heart of it. They're jealous because the other guys have the girl. It's totally simple when you think about it."

I was meditating on woolly mammoths, giant killer birds, jealous cavemen and the women they loved, when the manager halted before the two groups. His alarming redness of face made his salt-and-pepper moustache look positively alive, like a hairy insect riding across a lava flow.

"You must leave immediately, or I will call the police," he announced–to the wimps.

A woman's voice from the kitchen area shrieked.

"Oh my God! Nathan!"

As Nathan wheeled and sped off he stared daggers at the flustered young man with the angel fish in his drink.

"Get out of my restaurant!" he commanded, seizing the glass with the angel fish, while its straw swung around like a spar on a dinghy.

The barbarians pressed their advantage with alacrity.

"A sweet little fish."

"It will never know its happy home again."

"The merciless bastards!"

The defeated wimps rose like a flock of flamingoes, and the barbarians followed them. Weez and I were done eating, so we tossed twenty dollars on the table and headed out ourselves. I was moved by an impulse of sympathy for the girl in the red tank top. Exiting the men's room I saw her and asked if she was okay. But as I was speaking my gaze slipped, albeit very briefly, from her face to her chest.

"Don't hit on me, asshole," she said contemptuously.

A smiling young man seized the moment to hand me some Evangelical literature. I thanked him and found my way out the door, where Weez stood engrossed in another pamphlet from the Sins Forgiven Ministry. In the parking lot the barbarians were hectoring the girl as she climbed into an SUV. We stood at the fringe of their group and just stared at them.

When the SUV drove off they noticed us.

"What are you faggots looking at?"

I strode confidently over and handed the questioner the Word of the Lord.

"What the fuck is this?"

"God's kingdom is at hand!" I explained.

"What the fuck?" he countered, and shoved me back a step. "Fuck you, you fucking loser."

"Repent!" Weez cried, very loud. "Repent!"

Weez and I kept grinning like sacred idiots and they lost interest. They lurched into their pick-up trucks and roared off with a stinking belch of diesel.

I recounted what happened with the girl.

"You're leaving something out."

I confessed.

"You 'didn't mean anything by it!'" he laughed.

"Like you never look at a girl."

This stumped him. We had almost reached the hotel when he found his answer, like the right piece in a puzzle.

"I guess you have to know when to look."

Randy Pace scheduled a promo event for us at an independent re-tailer in Eugene, a place called Nimrod's. We arrived to find our new poster gracing the store window. I swallowed hard at the fact that Rex was twice as big as Hank and I. The manager, an ungainly sallow creature with huge hands, met us with a perfunctory grunt. Pat was his name. His sweaty hairy face seemed to be caving in, except the lips, which pushed outward their rubbery blue lobes like petals on a flesh-eating plant. For him it was the standard drill. He led us up to the makeshift stage, which was miked and ready to go before a crowd of about a hundred and fifty teens.

"Thirty minutes," Beazler reported. "No encores."

They were fairly sophisticated kids, too young for the club scene, too clever to behave themselves. They came bearing fresh tattoos, nose rings and ear rings, lipstick and nail polish and eyeliner. They brandished the usual lavish spectrum of hairstyles: long, bald, spiky, orange, blond, lime, blue, indigo, and black. There was no room to dance, so they watched us with sober overwrought faces. Back in Portland we'd performed a number of these shows, which were known to start off tense and hormonal. But warm applause makes everybody feel welcome and soon a young girl calls out.

"I love you, Rex!"

A tall woman with pale skin and long black hair, streaked slight-ly with silver, came by after the set to say hello. Over a sharp figure she wore a pinstripe suit and a white blouse. Her collar plunged to a depth of several buttons. Her nails were long and red. A young girl, maybe thirteen, dangled at her side.

"How are you?" the woman asked.

Her voice vibrated with the range of a cello. She had a promi-nent nose and strong eyebrows that gave her face a masculine quality. I couldn't decide if she was pretty.

"I'm Sharon," she said, very deliberately, like she was speaking in code. "And this is my daughter, Ophelia. We're your fans."

Ophelia had cut her brown hair very short, like a boy's. She was wearing black jeans, green Converse high tops, and a bright yellow shirt that said SMILE in soft black letters. She was pudgy but cute.

"Protecting Ophelia from the dangerous elements," I remarked.

"Ophelia," Sharon said, "this is the famous bass player, Freddie Fontane."

"His brother's keeper. And what grade are you in, Ophelia?"

"I'm going into ninth."

"Ophelia loves music. She plays the flute."

"Really?"

Ophelia burst into a grin, revealing the metal braces on her teeth. She mentioned that she used to play in her school orchestra.

"Here in Eugene?"

"No. In San Francisco. Mom and I have only been in Eugene a year. We're still getting used to it. We'll probably go back when Mom finishes with her appointment."

The girl spoke with a grown-up confidence that surprised me; but standing there in her black and yellow outfit she reminded me of a big bumblebee. Her mother was the queen. She was studying me. I glanced over at Rex, who sat on the stage amidst a worshipful throng. Hank had just given away a pair of drumsticks.

"Here, Ophelia, this is for you," I said, reaching into my case. "This is what I pick my brains with."

"Thank you," said Ophelia's mother.

She slipped a note into my hand as some other kids came over to meet me and the pair of them drifted away. It was near suppertime and we still hadn't done the soundcheck for our show that evening.

Driving by the university the bus driver shouted back at us.

"I hope none of you damned fools has drugs on him. There's a police car on our butt."

Sidney White was a gay black man. He used to carry 300 pounds on his lanky frame, but after a heart attack he'd whittled it down to

175. Behind his thick glasses he always seemed to be brooding. He wasn't going to be sidetracked by our nonsense. He didn't like to be called Sid. He was conservative in his opinions and when he discovered us watching porno on the bus, he forbade it.

"Not on my goddamn bus," he said.

Doubtless we would have ignored Sidney White had he been white. Being black we obeyed him for a day. And in fairness to us all, it wasn't just porno. It was Beazler's homemade selection, hardcore porno spatchcocked in between award-winning animated shorts. The *pièce de résistance* was a fanciful blend of the two genres, where Madonna gangbangs the Seven Days of Creation while singing "Like a Virgin" with a sneering English accent. In a satire of refreshing boldness in the face of corporate power (i.e. do not sue me, Medusa), she massages her fig-sized clitoris to turn on Light, follows up with an explosive cosmic enema, goes down on the Sun and the Moon, practices bestiality with various and sundry creatures on land, in the sea, and in the sky, and, practice making perfect, does it every which way with Old Adam before Eve comes along and cuts her rival's head off with a hedge-clipper. The video ends with Adam sneaking some head with the dissevered head. It won a $500 prize in Salt Lake City.

I glanced at the side-view mirror. Sure enough, there was a police cruiser stalking us. Then the cherry top started flashing.

As Sidney White pulled over I assessed my position. I was tired and I was hungry; but I had no drugs in my possession. The others worried me. Beazler said nothing. Rex appeared perfectly calm.

It was one of the local cops who boarded us. He looked like a young cowboy with a holster hanging from his hip and a ten-gallon hat with a star on it. He asked Sidney White for the vehicle registration, and Sidney White handed it over without a word.

"Good afternoon, gentlemen."

"Good afternoon, officer," Beazler said. "What can I do for you?"

We sat up in our seats, composed our faces in a respectful demeanor, and stuffed back the smirking beast. Hank put his Game Boy away. Weez put down his hot-rod magazine. No one wanted trouble. But in the closeness of the encounter we scattered enough scent to set the local hounds a-barking. It spread in a cloud around the invader's face. We didn't have to say a thing.

"Look," the cop began. "This is just a gentle warning. I'm not going to search you, but I want you to know that if you cross the line and we find out, you won't like the consequences."

We nodded like lilies in the field.

"Where you fellows coming from?"

"Portland," Beazler said. "We're touring the West Coast. This is a tour bus and this is the band. Would you like a CD?"

"No thanks," the cop said.

He looked us in the eye. He kept his poise. He didn't seem stupid or mean.

"I'm telling you for your own sake just stay out of trouble. Now I'm just going to ask you to sit here and relax for a few minutes while I check your registration. One of your brake lights isn't working."

After a quarter of an hour in limbo he handed the registration back to Sidney White.

"You playing in town tonight?"

"The 19th Hole," I told him. "Out on the golf course."

"It's a nice place," he said, waving his hand. "Have a good time."

"Fuck you, Wyatt Earp," Beazler said, as soon as the door closed.

It was 6:30 pm and we still hadn't reached the club. Sidney White started up the bus and another weary stretch of time ensued. Then he pulled back onto the shoulder.

"These directions are wrong. I followed them exactly, and there's no damn golf course in sight."

He appeared to have a point. The road had taken us into the middle of a forest. Grayish green fungus festooned the dense trees. Deeper in the remains of a wooden shack decayed amongst giant fronds.

"Where in the fucking universe is this?" Rex said.

"I'll turn around as soon as I can. We'll have to go back and ask somebody."

We pulled up at a gas station where the attendants had never heard of The 19th Hole. Luckily one of the kids from Nimrod's saw the tour bus. He offered to lead us and Sidney White followed him down a road that began twisting and turning around putting greens and fairways. I felt a wave of relief before the fatigue sucked us under. It would be dark in an hour and we hadn't even set up. My belly hung from my ribs like an empty kettle.

After the soundcheck it was too late to go out for dinner. Besides we might never find our way back. Beazler brought us cold chili in plastic ice cream cups.

"They say the microwave just broke," he explained.

"You try it first," Rex replied, skeptical of the lumpy ground beef and orange grease.

There was our poster on Main Street and here we were eating bad chili out of plastic ice cream cups. The dank dressing room further depressed us. The names of nameless bands adorned the walls. The beer sucked. You could feel the coils in the couch.

We vented our frustration on the opening act. They called themselves Ariel's Cave. In homage of what or whom I do not know. The Cave was a local band playing "for the experience." Possibly some of them had brought their girlfriends. Or maybe their baby sitters.

"You guys aren't as bad as you sound," Rex said, snatching the microphone and stepping boldly into the spotlight.

He slung an arm around the singer's neck. The young man smiled wanly. They'd just finished performing "another original." He was about a foot shorter than Rex and he must have doubted his senses.

"Can I borrow your bowler?" Rex asked, as he lifted the hat and placed it on his own head. "And your fake English accent? I've been looking all over for a fake English accent. *Look at me, I'm a hobbit!* Testing, testing. *Ta! Cheerio!*"

He galvanized the audience. Beazler took a quick poll and reported a ninety-five per cent approval rating of our action on stage. A focus group of "women who know the members of Ariel's Cave personally" proved to be surprisingly supportive. It turned out our insulting Ariel's Cave pleased them better than Ariel's Cave insulting them.

"Abort!" Rex shouted, inviting the crowd to join him.

"Abort!" I shouted into the next microphone.

Somebody, he looked uncannily like Beazler, hijacked the soundboard. He was brandishing the devil sign, index and pinky fingers.

"Abort!" he bellowed, leading the audience.

"Abort! Abort! Abort!"

The skinny frail guitarist, a kid maybe eighteen, started shaking. As he slunk off the stage I landed him a kick in the pants that made him hop. The audience rippled with delight.

At the bar liquor was flowing at 1:30 am. It was the hour of heroic drinking and inebriated trysts. Faces wandered into focus, their lineaments transfixed, then melted back into the crowd. Groups at tables reclined in the halflight, where swells of laughter bubbled and broke and sex streamed in powerful currents. Others drifted across the dance floor, eyes lit with the electricity that hung in the air. Even the girls were sweating. Their bodies were all over the place.

I was suspicious about the door receipts. It looked to me like there'd been at least five hundred people at the show; at ten dollars a head, I expected a take of about five grand. Rex vanished and Beazler said the take was half that.

"I'm going to talk to the guy," I told him.

"Don't you trust me, Freddie boy?"

"I think they're ripping us off."

I hurried away, but after a few steps I felt a hand squeezing my bicep. It was our tour manager.

"Listen. You better leave the guy alone. The take was a bit more than...All right. Rex cut a deal."

"You mean you and Rex blew the money on blow. And after what that cop said? You must be out of your fucking minds."

"Come on, Freddie. There's plenty to go around. You know what I mean. I've been very careful about things and we need to relax..."

"I knew we couldn't trust you."

"Look, Freddie. There are some fine-looking bitches here tonight..."

"I don't want to end up in jail, you fucking imbecile."

"You know that person?"

It was the woman from the record store. She stepped right up and patted me on the bottom. She wore a short black dress with high black boots and a spidery red wrap. She was smoking a cigarette.

"Hi," she exhaled. "How's Freddie, the famous bass player?"

Beazler sized up the situation and traipsed off without a word.

"Did you read my note?"

"No, I forgot."

I pulled the note from my vest pocket as she blew smoke in my face.

Freddie,

I want to be your whore.

Love, Sharon

A dark pleasure shot through me like a drug. She had a lot of nerve. But instead of getting excited, the devil of lust knew exactly what to do. He knew the brain is the only sinful organ in the body. So I replied with a kind of business proposition. The man next to us turned around and stared. I think he was shocked. I ignored him.

"All right," she said casually. "But I want you to see my paintings."

"All right."

When we got outside the night had barely cooled off. The moon was poking through shoals of dirty cloud. It flung a dollop of light onto the gray grass and scrub pine, and floated off.

"Can you handle a stick?"

She handed me the key to her black Boxster S and soon we were snaking around the deserted golf course. As I took in the feel of the car she reflected on the art world, which she described with jaded intimacy. The gallery owners were as bad as the museum curators. It was a bad business: stupid, vicious, and corrupt. They were all screwing each other, one way or the other. Most of the big exhibits were nonsense. They were a struggle between dull fashion and clever criminality. But for what it was worth, her paintings hung in museums all over the world. She'd eaten dinner the other day with the boss of a major London gallery.

"He just wanted sex. He was a real shit."

"You just want sex. I just want sex. That's what this is all about."

"You're a true artist."

"Did you shag him?"

"Yes. The fat slob."

She directed me past a fork in the road and we drove through town. People were drifting along the sidewalks, standing on corners, filtering in and out of bars. We passed the main drag, executed a series of turns, and raced down an unlit stretch of highway. When we hit a red light I looked her over.

"Do you often pick up men?"

"I could write a book about it. But you don't have to worry. I get myself checked."

"Do you have a thing for musicians?"

"You write the words and your brother writes the music. Isn't that it?"

I nodded as the light changed, accelerating in no time to sixty miles an hour. There was a ton of power under the hood.

"They were talking about it on the radio. You've been getting a lot of play."

"Glad to hear it."

"Do you like paintings?"

"Hopper."

"Hopper..." she mused, like someone weighing bullion in her hand.

"Are you into porn?"

"I adore it."

The night seemed bigger and darker as we got out of the car. Old trees flanked the enormous house in twisted shapes. I could feel them breathing. The noise of insects came booming in from all sides, and moths clustered under the front-door lights in fluttering columns.

The house was a Victorian mansion, a legacy to higher learning from some forgotten philanthropist. What was the source of his fortune? As Sharon paid the sitter I gazed at expensive objects, carved chairs and crystal cabinets, surreal paintings and baroque chandeliers, Persian rugs on honey-colored hardwoods. There were a grand piano in the music room, a vase of peacock feathers, and a golden horn in a glass case. Over it hung a manuscript by Richard Wagner with a daguerreotype of the composer.

Sharon lit another cigarette and offered me a drink. I asked for scotch on the rocks. She left the room exaggerating the sway of her hips and glancing over her shoulder. Returning she handed me a tumbler full of scotch and ice, single malt, smooth as the River Lethe. The gloomy immensity of the house agreed with her serpentine air, the musical depths of her voice, and the questionable beauty of her face, which was not young.

"Let me show you my paintings," she said, radiating smoke.

I followed her gliding figure up the broad central staircase to her studio, a high-ceilinged room illuminated by three tall standing lamps with brilliant globes, the nearest of which she switched off for a moment, before deciding to switch it back on. Otherwise the studio was sparsely furnished, with canvasses on easels or leaning against the walls. In the sharp glare I could see her thick lipstick was freshly applied. I could hear the bugs outside the open windows.

The paintings initially baffled me. I needed to stand back in order to see them. I liked the abstract perspectives, which had the tight logic of calculus. I observed that she worked with big canvasses.

"The size of windows," she said.

One painting was a zone of variable gray with a pure white disc in a corner. One showed a double rank of bodiless green wings mounting into the distance against an overwhelming yellow sky. The artist signed her work "Sharon O." etched in faint lines. Against the wall there rested a dark canvass where a convex grid of red bars made rounded rectangular spaces in which white filaments floated and curled. The filaments resembled the letters of an obscure alphabet.

"It's cool but I can't say why."

"Think of it as an escape from the body."

"What are these lines for?"

"The lines are bars. They represent a prison."

She walked behind me studying the canvas. I observed her professorial manner.

"Where is it?"

"It's everything you see."

"The whole world? You think the whole world is a prison?"

"I think our souls are uncreated. They don't belong in time. But the world...it tricks us. It needs us to buy into it. The trick is to escape the body with your soul intact."

"How do you do that?" I asked, sipping my scotch.

As she gazed at her work I felt absent from her view. She was intent on the painting. When she spoke again, it was an impersonal summation.

"You have to be stronger than your ego. The self has to be shattered to become a true self. It has to be broken, brought to heel. The true self rises from the ashes of the ego."

"How do you break the self?"

"Art is one way. When I paint I give myself up for something more. I lose all sense of time. The self is extinguished."

I sensed her attraction doubling, immersed in her weird, powerful paintings, and I thought I knew what she meant. Flush with drink, caught in the undertow of bass and drum, I knew what it was to be a wave breaking, dissolving out of time. Night after night, and others joined me.

"What's the other way?"

"Don't be stupid."

"How do you...without your body?"

"The body is the gun," she instructed me. "The soul is the bullet."

"And you fire the soul...into the yellow sky."

"Beyond the yellow sky. ...Please," she said curtly, avoiding my clumsy attempt at a kiss.

A few moments later she opened the door to an air-conditioned room with a large bed in a black metal frame, an antique gold loveseat, and a private bath. Along the far wall stood a wide-screen TV. She lifted a satin pillow from the bed and dropped it on the floor beside the loveseat.

"Sit here," she said, "and undo your belt."

She kneeled on the pillow, performing fellatio as she smoked another cigarette. She paused a moment to locate an ashtray. Then she resumed her performance, inhaling and taking me in her mouth, exhaling through her nose, deep-throating like a porn star.

At length she rose to extinguish her cigarette, which had burned down to a stub. Lingering before the mirror she removed the barrette from her long thick hair. She unzipped her boots and put them away. Then she played our CD and clicked on the screen.

"You're going to love this," she said, leaving the bathroom door open behind her.

A woman stood naked. She was outside, facing a wall. Her hips were beautifully curved, though she seemed slightly bow-legged in her stiletto heels. I hung my clothes on the back of the loveseat and relaxed on the bed, watching the movie. It was quality porn from Europe, probably the Czech Republic: the stuff America loves.

When Sharon returned she was naked. Her nipples were hard and her belly was tight. Her pubic hair was completely shaved.

"This is true hardcore," I said, nodding at the screen.

But a rap at the door surprised us. She pressed a finger to her lips; I had forgotten about her daughter, who must have been sleeping somewhere in the mansion. What was her name? As Sharon reached to unhook her robe I noticed a tattoo on the small of her back.

"Mommy..." the voice faltered against the sound of the CD player, one of those little marvels of technology, which fill a room so stunningly well.

Sharon pushed the door ajar so as to block ingress into the room and stepped out into the hallway. Her daughter's voice persisted in my mind. Ophelia. The woman kissed a man's ring and submitted to a collar and a leash. The man was handling her leash; she was crawling before him. The scene shifted to a bedroom. Ophelia's mother joined me on the bed as the sadism on the screen intensified. It was a sight that lifted my spirits. At least insofar as they resided in my crotch.

"Lucky girl," Sharon said, licking my chest like ice cream.

I rolled her onto her back and slid into her. She kept telling me to do it harder. I told her to shut up and went as hard as I could go. Wrestling a long time we drained all sympathy from our bodies as the mechanism took control. We didn't kiss. It was like her paintings: abstract, ascetic, severe.

"I hate a boy who can't fuck," she said, as I paused to catch my breath.

"Shut up."

"Fuck me, you little pig."

Observing the muscles of her face I still wasn't sure if she was beautiful or ugly. I fucked her and she sneered at me.

"Fuck your mamma, you little fucking pig."

I cuffed her flush on the cheek. She pulled me to her mouth

and our tongues entwined in a deep incestuous embrace. She dug her nails into my flesh until it hurt and I pushed her away. With her loins quartered she stared at the screen, masturbating like a zombie.

I took the occasion to remind her of the terms of our agreement. She made no bones about it. The devil of lust was in charge and I would have laughed but it seemed like we weren't even there, like we had disappeared behind the screen.

She was moaning or groaning as I fastened on the strange tattoo adorning her back. At first I thought it was a kind of ash-green ring. Then I saw it was a snake in the shape of a circle, with its tail fixed rigidly in its own mouth. I was mesmerized by it, engulfed by a sense of blank infinity, and when the moment dissolved my lust competed with my horror at the unforgiving sight of that snake.

SIX
The Fire

We were outside Oakland on the edge of a lifeless sprawling land-fill, being photographed. In one huge pit lay thousands of computer monitors, their screens cracked and splintered. Nearby a second crater gouged the earth, filled with oceanic lengths of frayed and mangled cable, which twisted in oracular silence. Unmarked green metal barrels stood here and there like dummies in a war game.

Lagging behind us Beazler was doing business on his cell. I gestured for him to dive into the nearest crater, and he responded with the finger. I have always admired "the finger." In the headlong roaring crush of late capitalism, the finger stands tall. The cheese stands alone but the finger stands tall. In a better world may they unite in solidarity.

The photographer wasn't happy with what he was getting. So he led us onto a field where industrial garbage sprouted like mutant cacti. In the middle distance rose a plateau of flattened cars.

"This place is definitely us, man," Hank said. "We ought to give a concert out here."

"Woodstock 3," Rex said.

"But Woodstock's in Ohio," Hank observed.

I said, "No, it's not. It's in New York."

"Oh yeah," Hank said, shaking his head. "I was thinking 'Four dead in O-hi-o.' What the hell was that crap anyway?"

"Nixon," I told him. "'Tin soldiers and Nixon's coming. They're finally on their own.'"

"Nixon went to Ohio?"

"He went to Ohio with Oswald's rifle. Started picking off hippies. Bang! Bang! Bang! Man were they pissed."

"Damn hippies," Hank said.

"That's why they always hated him," Rex said.

"Who was Nixon's VP?" Hank wanted to know.

I said, "Chef."

"What, from South Park?" Hank said.

"Of course. Chef from South Park. He was the first black Vice President. Only they caught him porking an intern. So somebody else got the position."

"Porking an intern," Rex said thoughtfully. "It was inevitable."

The photographer scowled into his expensive camera and directed us toward a crumbling ziggurat of tires. It was the kind of thing you looked at and thought: "Rex and The Brains." Meanwhile Weez returned from nowhere with a red, white, and blue serving tray. On the bottom it bore the patriotic slogan *America loves a Goldbrau.*

"It looks like an antique," he said. "I never heard of Goldbrau."

"What, you never saw the ad?" the photographer replied with annoyance. "It's something they put out last year. Took it off the market in six months. It flopped."

"Ah, Goldbrau," Beazler sighed. "The taste of cultivated rabbit urine."

"It's all in the marketing," Rex said.

The demand for our product was growing. *Painkiller* had sold over 150,000 units, which meant we'd generated our first million dollars in sales. But the song on the album getting the most airplay wasn't the title cut. It was a throwaway called "F.U. I Just Want To Get My Rocks Off," recorded in one take at the end of a long day in Burbank.

The morning of the shoot I woke up to the latest in a series of panic attacks. It was getting to be an unnerving routine. I lay in bed, collecting myself in scraps. As I stared at a flowery hotel curtain or the painted grille on a vent I fought off the grip of suffocation. I couldn't feel my hands or my feet. That morning I stood under a cold shower until the attack subsided.

It was 8:00 am when I fumbled around in my suitcase for something to wear. Rex was talking in his sleep.

"Worry, don't worry," he said.

As I headed out the door I saw Weez deep in slumber on the couch. He must have come back late, after everyone cleared out. I have no idea where he went on his own, if instinct compelled him to some anonymous exploit or if he just hung out with bikers and their ladies. He lay there, wrapped in a cool white sheet, with a peaceful look on his face.

The night before, the town reeked of piss. The new day broke with fine summer weather blowing in from the bay. The air was brisk and fresh. It must have rained.

"Hello, Sheila?"

"Freddie? Where are you?"

"San Francisco. South of Market."

"How's it going? Are you famous yet?"

"Well, there's posters of us in the record stores."

"Are you all right?"

"Fine. How's life in Portland?"

"Kind of slow. Didn't you call to confess?"

"What?"

"Didn't you call me to confess your sins?"

"I wouldn't know where to start. I'm afraid you wouldn't like me very much."

"Where are you now?"

"I told you. I'm in San Francisco."

"I mean, are you in a hotel?"

"No, I'm on a bench looking at some bums."

"Well, if I were you I'd say a prayer."

"You say one and I'll repeat it."

She started to recite the Hail Mary. A real golden oldie. But I found I couldn't repeat it.

"Hail Mary, quite contrary."

"Freddie, she'll pray for you."

"You believe that?"

"Yes, I do, cowboy."

After the shoot it was time for the drive down to Palo Alto. As we faced each other for another trip, Hank started talking about his family. He was under renewed pressure to return to college. He reminisced about his early years, a parade of nannies, private schools, soccer, and Ritalin. When he discovered his talent for drumming his father paid a man to build a soundproof bunker in the backyard.

I said, "What do they want you to do, become a plastic surgeon?"

"It's a funny life," he said. "It never turns out like you expect."

I was wondering whose life he meant when Weez asked a question.

"Freddie, what happened to that girl you went out with? The one at the funeral..."

"Oh yeah," Rex said. "What was her name?"

"Her name's Sheila. I called her today."

"You what?" Rex said, as Sidney White crept along in the middle lane.

"Yes. You see, I wanted to talk to her."

"Why?"

"What's she like?" Weez said.

"Well, I'd have to say she's pretty religious."

"I believe in God," Rex said.

I said, "No you don't."

"I just don't believe in traditional religion. We wouldn't have all these wars if it wasn't for traditional religion."

"Tell me one thing you believe in," I said. "Give me one article of faith."

"My own faith?"

"I'm listening."

"I believe that God is in all things, that we're no different from any other animal. That's just bias. We all eat, shit, and have sex. We're all made from the same materials–stars billions of years old. We're all made of God."

"You never felt that human beings are unique?"

Just then a driver talking on a phone grazed the car below my window. There was an angry honk as she angled down the exit ramp without pausing. There were kids in her backseat.

"There's intelligent life all over the universe."

"How come we've never heard from it?"

"You're missing the point. We're made of DNA, like every other living thing. DNA is a molecule, like H_2O. We're not unique."

"Monkeys don't write symphonies."

"They write rock songs," Hank said. "'I'm a Believer'..."

"That was Neil Diamond," Beazler corrected him.

I said, "There's nothing like the human brain out there and you just don't want to face it. There are no Martians, no Vulcans, no Star Wars...it's all make-believe. And they've never made life in a test tube. Think about it. There's an incredible difference between studying DNA and actually creating it."

"I don't believe in Martians, I don't believe in Star Wars, I don't believe in test tubes..."

It was Beazler riffing on the Plastic Ono Band.

I said, "You know he's actually got a point for once."

"Freddie, you're wrong," Rex said. "It's just arrogance to think that we're alone or even that what matters to us today is going to matter to anyone in a million years. The truth is we're evolving. You've got to see the larger picture."

"So you believe in a God that's evolving?"

"Yes I do."

"So could it change into its opposite?"

"What is she?" Rex asked, changing the topic.

"What religion? She's a Catholic."

"How can you defend those priests?" he demanded. "After what they did to those little boys? 'Bend over, child. I bugger thee in the name of the Lord. Amen.' You know how many lives they wrecked? I mean really totally wrecked. The Catholics ought to give it up for Chrissake."

"Not Sheila Corcoran?" Beazler said. "She's not worth your time, Freddie."

"Keep it to yourself, fat boy."

He seemed to heed my advice. But when the conversation flagged, he spoke again.

"Remember Johnny D? When was it? I remember walking in on them at his place. They were on the floor. He was fucking her like a dog. God, was she embarrassed.

"Nice tits," he added, bouncing his palms in front of his chest.

"Fuck you, Captain Asshole."

"Okay, Freddie. Be that way."

When Rex made a few calls to arrange a victory tour for himself around Palo Alto, Weez decided not to join him. He'd noticed in the paper that a blues band he liked was playing in the area. I decided to stick with Weez.

"Who are these guys?" I asked him.

"What, you never heard of The Lubbock Blues Band? 'Don't You Leave Me Dying on Your Doorstep?' 'The Girl Next Door to the Girl Next Door?' 'I Used To Be the Lord Before I Was a Loser?' Man, they're huge."

We borrowed Adrian's red Audi and drove out by Edward Teller's house (I used to cut the old man's lawn–very nice). After hearing about Teller and the H-Bomb Weez confessed he'd taken a two-year degree at a community college. They offered a year-long course in recording technology.

"What was your grade?" I laughed.

"B plus. Mr. McGreary's class. I screwed up the first term but aced the second."

"That's pretty good."

"McGreary came to see us last winter."

"What'd he say?"

"Oh, he twiddled a few knobs."

"Yeah?"

"And after he left I changed them back," he grinned roguishly. "I noticed old McGreary has trouble sorting out the midrange."

We had well over an hour to kill, so we drove down Palm Drive to visit the well-manicured campus of Stanford University. We parked the car and found ourselves strolling past the sandstone arcades of the deserted Inner Quad.

"It's quite a place...Did you learn anything?"

As we walked along the answer finally occurred to me.

"Fogballs."

"What?"

"I learned the art of fogballs."

"I never heard of a fogball."

"A fogball is a meaningless remark that everyone tolerates. The classic all-time fogball is *it's all relative*. But there's also *our differences will save us* and *change is good*. If someone disagrees with you, you can always smile and say *we'll have to agree to disagree*."

"Brilliant."

"There was a speech code," I explained. "And I think people just gave up on trying to say anything real."

In White Plaza summer students were lounging around the fountain. We sat down on a bench and some hungry sparrows came by. Everything was quiet except the birds and the fountain.

"No one I knew was really happy here. Don't get me wrong, we weren't especially unhappy, either. We were into instant messaging. We just hung out, did homework, hooked up. The usual routine."

The sparrows were hopping in and out of each other's way, fluttering small wings. I stomped my boot and off they sailed.

"I knew a lot of women. We acted like pals. Now I wonder where they are."

We just sat there. The sky was starting to change.

"I suppose you've never heard of the great Frantz Fanon. He used to teach here. He taught a lot of people what to think. Anyway, they said it was like I'd learned nothing at all."

"Who?"

"I got into an argument one time with a couple of my professors. It was at a party. I said I liked books with a good plot."

"Why else would you read a book?"

The sunlight was pouring off the red dome of Hoover Tower. You could see for miles up there.

"You don't want to know."

"Is that a fogball?"

"I can't help myself. It's automatic."

The Post House was an old saloon. Some leathery coot tucked away in the hills might recall the years of Prohibition when the place was a speakeasy and horses munched their oats alongside Mr. Ford's jalopies. The building itself made no pretense to historical charm. It was a whitewashed box with black shutters on the upstairs windows.

We sat at the bar as the band went on. At first I thought the sound system wasn't very good. Then it became clear that the soundman was inept. Feedback jolted the singers. The drums vibrated like a jackhammer. The keyboard disappeared, peeped out its head, leaped into the air, and drowned. The Lubbock Blues Band was in trouble.

I watched with amusement as our skinny soundman wedged his body through the press of people to the soundboard, where he made a number of practical suggestions to the apprentice on duty. After a few adjustments the high end came into focus and the bass grew more distinct. The feedback stopped. The keyboard steadied itself. I saw the lead singer give Weez an appreciative thumbs up.

While Weez extended his holiday at the soundboard I shouted at the bartender for directions to the men's room. He shouted back it was through the double doors and down the hall. I had trouble locating the double doors, which were hidden behind the stage. On entering the hall I bumped into a young man wearing a cowboy hat. It was a dude named Edgar Messinger I knew from high school. He was famous for winning a truck our senior year. It was a beautiful red pick-up. I was glad to see him but it was too loud to say much so we slapped each other on the back and went our separate ways. The hall was dark and low. Finally it delivered me to the right door, next to a janitor's closet, next to an unmarked door that was bolted.

Like other men who gratify their vanity in the smallest departments of life, I have always prided myself on having a capacious bladder; and as I moseyed up to the ancient latrine I sensed the possibility of a new record. So I put my hands on my hips and pee'd like John Wayne's horse. Then I swaggered over to the mirror and admired my photogenic face. So what if Rex's picture was bigger. Edgar Messinger had bought a copy of *Painkiller*. He said it was great. I thought that somebody must have come in quietly behind me with a cigarette because there was a smell of smoke.

When I exited the men's room the smell was much stronger. The music stopped and suddenly voices were shrieking. Then I heard a sound like drums tumbling over and people started pushing past me with vivid distorted faces. Somebody opened the door to the janitor's closet and screamed.

I still couldn't fathom what was going on. Then I saw a ripple of flame near the stage. The long low hall was crowded with frightened refugees and somebody was pulling frantically at the bolts on the unmarked door. It swung open into the alien calm of the parking lot.

Almost immediately the rush of bodies exhausted itself. Outside men and women were wailing and weeping. Overhead dense smoke curled like wings, rising from the building and into the starry night. A big guy, the drummer, waded back into the smoke calling the name "Sonny." I followed him. At the double doors I could hear tortured voices but it was too smoky to see. I took off my tee-shirt and tried breathing through it. The drummer and I were shouting through a curtain of flame.

"This way! The exit's over here! Behind the stage!"

"Sonny!"

"Weez! Tim Cove!"

A bewildered couple made it through, then a woman stooped and sobbing, then a final straggler, coughing and gagged with smoke, and then my shirt caught fire. The whole stage was burning. We had to back off from the barbed unyielding heat.

I ran to the front of the building where groups of people stood frozen in sheets of flickering light. Their staring faces mirrored shock. The saloon was a furnace and I could smell the unspeakably horrible. A few more made it out, hacking smoke, scarred and singed. I was deadlocked. The main floor had no windows. A hundred people were trapped.

The fire continued to roil and crackle. In a burst of obscene hideous laughter it tore through the roof and unleashed a demented wailing that rose and fell on waves of flame. Specters wandered here and there beside me, crying out.

"Donna! Sweetheart!"

"Weez! Tim Cove!"

When the first fire engine arrived they discovered the fire hydrant didn't work. The men got out their axes. But there was nothing they could do. Lights were flashing from police and fire vehicles. I saw a great tall man drop his axe and stoop to the ground, vomiting.

"Tim! Where are you?! Tim?..."

Someone wrapped a blanket over me. I tried calling Rex but his cell was off. Then I tried Beazler.

"Hi, Freddie. What's going on?"

"There's been a fire."

"Shit. Are you all right?"

"I can't find Weez."

"Where are you?"

"Tell Rex I'm at the Post House. Come right away."

I awoke in my old bed with a delay of consciousness. Then I saw Rex sitting at the desk with the aquarium behind him. The aluminum reflector slanted into the empty tank.

"Is he dead?"

"Looks like it.

"Jesus Christ," he said, slumping in the chair and cradling his head in his hands.

Hank waited in the kitchen. His face was pale and strained. I poured a glass of water from the refrigerator door, staring at the slogan posted there:

A PEOPLE'S VICTORIOUS FIGHT
CONSECRATES ITS RIGHTS.
Frantz Fanon

I sat at the kitchen table. The familiar floor had a bright polished appearance. I lifted the kitchen phone.

"I need to reach the Coves."

"We already did," Rex said. "They're flying down today."

"Who spoke with them?"

"I did," Beazler said, making my stomach wince. "It was my responsibility. You don't have to worry. I was very professional. There was nothing you could do."

"That's enough, John," Rex said. "Now listen, Freddie. We've got to keep going. And Beazler's right about one thing. You're in no way responsible for what happened last night. Nobody is. He wanted to go and you went with him."

"I have to reach the Coves."

"Now listen," he began again. "We can't cancel tonight. Everyone we know will be there. We have to play."

A kind of warp, like a bend in a funhouse mirror, seemed to exile our bodies and their emotional burden, which had nothing to do with our music's ironic edge. During a lugubrious pause, oozing to the brim with melodrama, Rex told the audience what had happened. Everybody knew about the Post House. But none of us knew what gesture to make or symbol to hold on to.

That night I noticed for the first time the perfect calm that floats above the audience in a large theater, behind the bright shaft of the spotlight. I felt weightless, communing with that hovering negative. It was a threshold that offered sanctuary, a dark heaven where my fears were projected and dissolved until all personal feeling and even death itself seemed to be extinguished.

I drove back alone to Penelope's house and fell asleep in an armchair watching coverage of the fire, the impending war, and a corrupt priest who'd fled from Boston to San Francisco. At six in the morning the phone rang.

"Good morning, Freddie, this is Vernon Cove."

"Good morning, Mr. Cove."

"Freddie, can I come by and pick up my son's belongings?"

"No, please, Mr. Cove. I mean, let me bring them by. Where are you?"

"I'm at the Red Lion. I'm in the coffeeshop."

"I'll be there in half an hour."

The poor man was sitting by himself in the empty dining room. Carrying his son's suitcase I joined him in his booth. The suitcase was heavy and I placed it at his side. There was one other customer, reading the morning paper.

It was difficult to hear everything Mr. Cove said. He told me the police had the site cordoned off. He couldn't even get close. His voice kept slipping into inaudibility and he hadn't slept since Beazler's phone call.

"You drove out there?"

"They wouldn't let me in. So I pulled off the road and walked. But I couldn't get in. They stopped me."

The hostess came by with coffee and scalded Mr. Cove's hand. He blinked with pain, raked an ice cube from his water glass, and pressed it to his skin.

"They say it'll be weeks before they identify all the bodies."

"How long are you going to be in town?"

The other customer departed and left his newspaper behind.

Mr. Cove was looking at his son's suitcase as the busboy came to clean the vacant booth.

"How long did you say?"

"Weeks before they know."

Then he mumbled something about The Lubbock Blues Band. He couldn't believe it was The Lubbock Blues Band. He was playing them down at the shop Saturday morning.

"Sonny Jackson...they say he also died."

"The singer?"

"Sonny played the bass."

"Someone was calling out 'Sonny' when the fire started. He was calling Sonny and I was calling Tim. We were in the hall together. We had to get out because of the heat."

"God."

"Can I get you anything, Mr. Cove?"

"No, that's fine, son. You better go."

I wanted to comfort him, to touch him. But I hardly knew the man.

SEVEN
Sons and Daughters

The last night of the *Painkiller* Tour Randy Pace crashed the scene in a brassy sports coat with an American flag pin on the lapel. It was all arranged. We were going to play the Staples Center in August. Earlier that week "F. U. I Just Want To Get My Rocks Off" cracked the Top Forty. As caterers swept in with champagne and caviar Randy Pace said the company was delighted. Crocodile wanted us to enjoy our success the right way. He was there to help.

It is well known that in states of malicious excitement the male chimpanzee will hurl handfuls of excrement at his business associates. That is a gene I regret losing in the wilderness of evolution.

"It's good to see you smiling, Freddie," Randy Pace said.

He strongly advised us to stay in LA. For one thing it was imperative that we shoot a video to support the single. For another we were California boys. There was no one there for us in Oregon. We needed to leave the past behind. He would find us comfortable housing and an excellent rehearsal space. In the meantime we had a five-star hotel and a few days rest on our hands.

He was sorry to hear about Tim Cove. His jowls thickened like a dolorous pudding.

"This kind of thing happens far too often in our business."

"He was a nice guy," Beazler said sorrowfully. "I'll miss him."

A few days later I found myself in the neighborhood of an old Spanish church. A plump Mexican nun in a habit held the door for me. She was locking up, but she smiled and told me to please come in and pray. I followed her in, breasting the musty heat. Still white flames burned in a blue light. High above the altar Christ swam on a giant crucifix. The nun retired with a polite bow when the thought occurred to me that I needed to attend the funeral. So I reached for my cell. The daughter who answered said both her parents were out. The nun reappeared, looking upset. I told the girl who I was and asked if they had found her brother's body. She told me they had. The nun started screeching in Spanish. She shooed me all the way down the nave, out the door, and then stamped on the steps like she was chasing a pigeon.

I planned on attending the funeral alone, but when I arrived in Portland I decided to stop by Sheila's apartment and say hello. She came down in jeans and a T-shirt. Her surprise at my appearance set off bells of doubt.

"Sorry I didn't call. Should I go?"

"No. Please come in. But there's somebody visiting."

In the apartment I encountered a stocky young man in a blue blazer and khaki trousers. He stood by a table lamp, which poured a circle of light onto a thick scroll of blueprints.

"Freddie Fontane, this is Eliot Buckley. Eliot, this is Freddie Fontane."

"Hi, Freddie. A pleasure to meet you."

His plummy voice had the dual effect of pleasing himself and annoying me. A weak handshake compounded the suggestion that I was intruding on his particular turf. With his blond beard and Ivy League deportment his style might interest a woman.

"Eliot was showing me the designs for a new building."

"I just got the good news," he said. "The competition was fairly intense. It's only my second building downtown.

"What do you do, Freddie?" he asked, as I stood silently by with Sheila smiling on us both.

"Nothing, Eliot. I was just dropping by to ask for sympathy."

"Freddie's a musician."

"A rock star?"

"A porn star."

"Oh, how interesting," he said, smiling briefly. "In what band may I ask?"

"The North American Man-Boy Love Association. Have you heard of us? We're huge in Boston."

"Umm, would you like a drink, Freddie? Eliot and I were just having some iced tea. There's fresh mint. It's really very nice."

"No, I'd better go."

She'd been drinking iced tea and talking to a normal person. Now there I was knocking on her door like Gilgamesh after the death of Enkidu.

Maybe the most daring thing about Christianity, said the young priest, is its faith in the material resurrection of the body. Timothy's body, which had been destroyed by fire, would be made new at the time of the Second Coming. It would be perfected, a perfect instrument of the spirit, raised above the weakness of the earthly body. But the essential thing is that you would recognize Timothy as himself. You would recognize him and rejoice.

He walked back to the lectern and found the page he wanted.

"It was ordained for human kind to pass through the apocalypse before the Second Coming could occur. But the apocalypse is not a single event happening only at the end of time. It is an event that echoes from its source throughout our lives. Sacred history is universal. It exists alongside secular history. Now here is a passage I have thought much about. It is, I admit, a difficult passage. Some might say it is inappropriate for us today to hear such things. But let us consider it as best we can: 'The first angel blew his trumpet, and there came hail and fire, mixed with blood, and they were hurled to the earth; and a third of the earth was burned up...' That, my brothers and sisters, is the start of the apocalypse, the fire that burns away the veil. Mystics tell of passing through, beyond the burning fire, to glimpse the truth behind our world. Now, I believe, and I believe it with no forced zeal or cold conviction, that Timothy in the end came to God. At this altar he was confirmed Timothy Daniel and now I see that his confirmation name was beautifully chosen. For Daniel was a prophet and one like the Son of God. Daniel tells of the righteous walking 'in the middle of the fire, and they are not hurt...' What could that mean, 'they are not hurt?' The way for us to understand and to live with Timothy's death, this shocking and unthinkable loss, is to remember that our world is not the only world. Faith tells us there is a God, beyond the circle of our understanding. But it is salutary at this time to recall that considerable testimony exists, the report of good witnesses in the plain light of day, confirming for us that Jesus of Nazareth died and rose on the third day and walked among the living. They were not mystics who reported the empty tomb. The resurrection was not a symbol to the first Christians. It was and it remains a remarkably sturdy fact. Family and friends, we can hope with a good hope that Timothy is not hurt, that he has passed through the fire to be with God, where he awaits the Second Coming of our Lord, Jesus Christ. May God have mercy on his soul, and on our souls.

"Peace be with you."

Heavy clutter of marble angels awaited our coming in the warm afternoon. New rows of headstones glistened with a fine finish, like they would be going on sale soon. I found a peaceful spot behind a hedge and wept. Then I noticed a picture of a little girl, mounted on a stone. She was eleven or twelve when she died. Her eyes were blue. The hedge and the tomb made a three-walled temple where I pondered the whole intolerable business, concluding with a shudder of disbelief, after which came nothing, and then a single winding note, a whistle of faint light that called my attention to the grass beneath my feet. What, I wondered, did the grass have to do with it?

Mrs. Cove was catatonic. She could barely lift her feet to walk. She squeezed my hand and sobbed. Later that evening, when people were used to me, they started asking questions. They wanted to know what Tim's job was. He was a sound engineer. I explained that it was a craft, and that he never missed a cue. What exactly was a cue? Say the vocal needed an effect, an echo for instance, at a certain point in a song. He would control the effect. Or say we had to play a small room one night, and a big room the next. He had to make adjustments for the type of space. It was his job to check the acoustics, the way that sound moves around a room. If the sound was muddy, he cleared it up. He had to distinguish and balance lows, mids, and highs, for example, bass guitar and bass drum, rhythm guitar and vocal, cymbals and harmonics. There could be acoustic shadows and other problems.

Mr. Cove wanted me to stay until the end. He got out the booze and told me to recount the story of his son's last hours. I thought why bring it up? Then I remembered the feedback from the stage monitors. How Weez had gone off to save the band. The Lubbock Blues Band must not have had their regular sound man with them. The apprentice couldn't work the board.

"He was doing what he loved," a middle-aged man said.

Struck by the family resemblance I replied, "Yes. That's very true."

There was quiet in the room.

I said, "He was extremely good at his job...I don't think I appreciated him enough."

"You were his friend," Mr. Cove said. "He always spoke of you as his friend."

How he managed to say that I'll never know. We drank some more and talked about the fire.

Sheila called to suggest a picnic at the beach. She made some sandwiches and I drove us in my rental, a blue Ferrari convertible with a six-speed manual transmission. It felt good to drive to the coast. Sunset Highway is a big country road, and the coupe handled well, gripping the road as we accelerated through a wide reach of meadow.

"That's fast enough for me, cowboy," Sheila said as the speedometer hit ninety.

The land that way is checkered with family farms and new technology firms. These corporate armies pitch their chrome pavilions boldly on the grassy heights, and join in battle on the information superhighway. In other valleys we passed small herds of cattle cropping the thick grass, and I caught sight of a pair of horses, blond palominos cantering over a ridge. Very pretty animals. Eventually we reached a fork in the road where the rolling country yielded to steep hills and old-growth forest.

Sheila had in mind a beach on the Washington coast, near a town called Oysterville.

"Oysterville," I repeated, savoring the name. "I like oysters."

We approached a huge green bridge, four windy miles of steel and concrete stapling together Oregon and Washington. Below us the Columbia poured its current westward, scenting the Pacific. We crossed the wide flood and followed Route 101 to the narrow cape where the village of Oysterville lies anchored against the tide.

"So how did you hear about this place?"

"I went to a wedding out here last year. A girl Jack and I knew. Meg O'Donnell. She married some guy she met in Cancún."

As we reached the cape, acres of beach grass spread out along the road. Slender trees rose in patches among the pulses of water in countless shiny inlets.

"They threw one hell of a party," she said. "It was the funniest wedding I've ever seen."

"Ha-ha funny or strange funny?"

"Both, I suppose. But you have to know Meg. She was always a headstrong girl. When we were kids, maybe thirteen, we used to hang out in a group in the cafeteria and she had this momentous vision, that we needed to paint our rooms a particular light shade of green, honeydew I think it was."

"Celestial Melon."

"It was supposed to be the most peaceful of all colors. So we bought brushes and paint and went to work. It took us all summer to finish. Then Iraq invaded Kuwait.

"Do you know when Earth Day is?"

"February 2nd, I believe..."

"No, Freddie, that's Groundhog Day. Funny, I can't remember when Earth Day is. Anyway, Meg and I were on the Student Council and she loved to lecture about the pollution we were all causing–even our breath. At last she got permission from the principal and they bussed us off to a disused lot. It was owned by the city. We spent the day clearing the ugliest trash I've ever seen–tons of it. The rest of us wore gloves and goggles, but Meg didn't do the dirty work, she just directed."

"That's the way it always is."

"And then she got really mad because we wouldn't stay late... Now what was after Earth Day?"

"Global warming?"

"No...I think it was vegetarianism. That was Meg at her absolute worst. She descended screeching like a harpy, crying 'Meat is murder! Meat is murder!' Then she'd pound her fists on the table and hop up and down like a deranged little orc. It got to the point where we had to keep a look-out.

"You know what she called Burger King?"

"What?"

"'Murder King.'"

"Like MacBeth...Ronald MacBeth."

"Later she expressed some regrets. We saw each other occasionally on campus, though we were never really close. It surprised me to be invited to her wedding, but she said she wanted to have me and Jack there for old time's sake. She was getting married on the beach. I remember telling her it might be a little difficult, what with the wind and all, but she had her mind made up, being Meg. It turned out to be a lovely day and everything seemed fine. She wore a beautiful orange sari with a ceremonial cape–she'd converted to Buddhism..."

"Isn't the University of Portland a Catholic school?"

"That's what happens at Catholic schools. A friend of mine called our class 'a fine budding crop of Nietzschean Buddhists.'"

I was digesting this unusual phrase as we passed the signs for Oysterville. We were a week ahead of the fair. They were going to have the world-famous chickens: the ones who play tic-tac-toe.

"So the bride and groom were standing halfway down the pier, a breakwater built of huge blocks of stone, with this petite monk from Tibet saying the words of the ceremony. Nobody could hear him. The groom wore a silver tuxedo with a bright orange boutonniere and white shoes. He was tall as a giraffe. She wore a sea-shell necklace, her orange sari, and heels. Oh, I forgot, as they walked onto the breakwater her brother played 'Here Comes the Bride' on the bagpipes."

"Here comes the bride of Frankenstein..."

"Well, the groom lifts a big fat diamond ring high into the air so everybody can see it sparkle, only he drops it. Poor Meg is hobbling around searching for her ring when suddenly the wind gusts up and *whoosh* grabs her cape and sweeps her straight into the ocean."

"Jesus."

"It was like the hand of God! The groom just stood there at the edge of the rock, staring at the water. I think he was stoned. The little monk ran up and down the pier whirling his arms like propellers. It looked like he was going to take off. The next thing I knew Jack was racing down the breakwater in his underpants. He dives into the ocean and fishes out poor Meg..."

"Jack to the rescue. Did they finish the wedding?"

"Meg felt she had to. They'd spent all that money and I think the monk needed to be in California the next day. So she got married on the beach in her blue jeans."

I slowed for the exit.

"It lasted a week," she said as I studied the signs.

"The party?"

"Nope. The marriage."

Oysterville is a pleasant sea town with a small white church, a graveyard, and a picturesque fishing fleet. Main Street looked hospitable, but it wasn't for us. On an unpeopled stretch of beach we ate our picnic and lay for a good long while gazing at the wind-picked sky. Then I kissed her lips. It was a good kiss and we went for a walk. Some of the weeds had a reddish, fiery appearance. If you touched them white moths flew out. The surf fell back for quite a distance and exposed a shelf of tidal pools, the dwelling of pale green sea-anemone, purple starfish, and black mussels, who make their beds on the clustered rocks. Sea-cucumbers strewed the way amidst the daily wreckage of the Pacific, molted claws and shattered shells. The gulls strutted about like pompous monarchs. It was constantly blowing.

We walked a mile or two, past the breakwater where nemesis awaited the headstrong bride, past a group of children flying kites, to the base of a dark promontory that jutted out into the waves. It formed a natural limit, and when we finally reached it we were surprised to find a small monument sheltering under one of its crumbling ribs. It was a bronze plaque, thickly encrusted with verdigris, screwed onto a three-foot tall slab of granite. All we could decipher of the embossing were a few words, "sighting," "Japanese," and "1942."

"Fort Stevens is just south of here," Sheila said. "The Japanese attacked it in World War II. It's right at the mouth of the Columbia."

"No way."

"Really. They attacked it with a submarine. It's in Astoria, near the bridge."

"Damn."

I grew aware of a road dead-ending behind us. Thirty yards

away a couple of kids pulled up in a jeep. They kicked back in their bucket seats and lit up a joint. They looked like clean-cut high school boys. They were blasting the radio and as the pungent scent of marijuana tinged the salt air it mixed with a drumbeat I recognized. Then a chord detonated and Rex started singing. The vibration of the bass actually loosened a layer of rock above our heads. A cascade of tiny fragments rained down near our feet and for a moment I had a fantastic image of the cliff collapsing, burying me and Sheila along with the monument.

"Isn't that Rex and The Brains?" she said.

"It's the national anthem," I said. "Makes you love your country, doesn't it?"

"Funny boy."

Her auburn hair was streaming in the wind. I held her hand as we turned to go back. The boys drove off in their jeep, scattering the song behind them, and the pounding of the waves was like the pounding of my heart.

"IS THERE ANY ALTERNATIVE TO BLIND ACCEPTANCE OF THIS SITUATION?" The words of my old friend Professor Bogardus came thundering back. They were the constant refrain in his seminar on the Enlightenment. They rang in my head like a chorus of tragic Greeks. But as always I was uncertain of their application.

The house was lonely. There were no visitors, no mail, and no Jim Dandy. Immediately upon my arrival I'd noticed his absence. The grinning dog had wandered off, gone to convert the heathen. I felt dispirited. During a search of the house I confronted the situation as it flashed before my eyes, grew dark, flashed less brightly, then darkened less intensely, until it left me rambling through an internal twilight that seemed deeply familiar.

I got Ellen's answering machine and hung up. Next, I elected to have lunch. I'd stopped at the deli and picked up a half-pound of good roast beef, a few kaiser rolls, mayonnaise, muenster cheese, and tomatoes. Sheila would take the trouble to put lettuce on a sandwich; but that meant washing the lettuce, a step I was never prepared to take. Lettuce is demanding: its natural enemy is the rabbit. Do you see a connection?

I slathered on the mayo, piled up the cool roast beef, added two square slices of muenster, two round slices of beefy tomato, a sprinkle of salt and pepper, and thought about Iraq. Then I poured myself a tall glass of milk. On the back porch it was a fine summer day. No birds troubled the sky with their calls and feathers, a fact I was grateful for, no omens for me, please—I'd learned my lesson. The caretaker had left hours ago and the herd was drifting sunken headed towards the electric fence, close to where I was sitting. They were true Aberdeens, black and ponderous. One of the cows happened to lift her rheumy eyes and stare straight at me.

"IS THERE ANY ALTERNATIVE TO BLIND ACCEPTANCE OF THIS SITUATION?" I reflected, biting off a piece of roast beef.

I took another bite of my sandwich, and another, and washed it all down with cold milk. The cows were flicking their tails and munching the grass. A breeze wafted over with an aroma of fresh dung. "Bravo!" I cried, and several animals, the smarter ones, I imagine, looked over. "IS THERE ANY ALTERNATIVE TO BLIND ACCEPTANCE OF THIS SITUATION?" they seemed to say.

I tried my sister again and she answered with a dubious hello, ready to brush off the sales parasite. A child wept in the background, so I got straight to the point. I asked if I could stay at her house. No, that wasn't all.

"She's the girl you told me about?"

"Yes, I guess we'd need separate rooms. Do you think you have enough space?"

"I have to check with Manny but I think you can use the guest house. It's small but it'll do. She could probably sleep upstairs in the spare bedroom. Ask her if she can help with the campaign. She can visit the website. Better yet, is she good with children? That would really help. The pace around here is nuts. There are meetings in the basement until four in the morning. Manny has given up sleep."

The next day I located the website on Sheila's laptop: *Emmanuel Mantica for US Congress.*

"He's my brother-in-law," I announced with no clear sense of what I was doing.

"He's pro-life...He and Ellen both are."

Sheila started reading. She had just finished a shower when I rang the doorbell. Her hair was dripping wet.

"Huh," she said.

Beads of sweat broke out on my forehead. The whole falling-in-love shtick seemed retro and ridiculous, but it was still possible to look at things pragmatically: either I was going to pursue a course of action that promised some good in the end, or I was going to migrate to LA and dive like a swan, or a shark, make that a rat, into the club scene. Sheila was studying me with amusement.

"Let me get this straight. You want me to quit my job, go down to LA, work on your brother-in-law's campaign, baby-sit his kids, and live in his house. On what basis may I ask?"

I kissed her on the mouth and ran my hand through her wet lustrous hair. It became hard to separate and as we fell on the couch we nearly knocked over the vase of roses I'd brought the day before.

For Mass Sunday morning Sheila wore a blue summer dress. A simple white belt caught the charm of her figure. The news was that her father had invited us to lunch. She kissed me on the lips and mentioned his friend would be joining us, a woman named Roseanne Phillip.

"You look kind of pale."

"Does this mean you'll go to LA?"

"Ask me again after lunch."

"If your father doesn't kill me..."

"Freddie..."

"And then eat me."

The Corcoran house was on NW Savier over by Forest Park. The front room was handsomely appointed, with a leather sofa and chairs and tall bookcases laden with art and books and pictures. Above the mantelpiece hung a portrait of a woman I seemed to recognize. She looked about twenty-five. A hint of laughter played in her eyes and lips, which curled in mischievous loveliness, as though she was pretending to be grave and serious to please the artist.

Ben Corcoran and his friend Roseanne Phillip came in from the kitchen. I recognized him from the funeral at Saint Mary's. He was middle-aged and clear-eyed, with a quiet, intelligent manner that drew my attention. She managed a thin layer of charm over her prim and officious personality. Both had their sleeves rolled up.

We walked through the kitchen to an indoor patio or sun room, which opened onto a terraced garden basking in sunlight. The table in the patio was set for four. In its center stood a blue vase with bright marigolds. Ben and Roseanne brought in plates of steamed asparagus, wild rice, and baked chicken. A final touch was a thick hot loaf of homemade bread.

After grace Ben raised a question about the Divinity School his daughter was planning to attend. He wanted to know if the classes were taught in Latin. She said they were restoring two courses on the Church Fathers to be taught in that language.

"It must be difficult to translate modernity into Latin. How would you say 'Disneyland?'"

"Disneyland? Well, how about *terra mira*, or *mundus mirabilis*? But that's why they're starting with Augustine and Jerome. Disneyland isn't mentioned in *The City of God*."

"I must admit," Roseanne Phillip commented, "that I am absolutely appalled at the state of our popular culture."

"What do you do for a living?" I asked.

"I am a clinical psychologist."

"Oh, my mother's a psychologist. She's a professor."

"May I ask her name?"

"Penelope Driver."

"Good Lord. You're the son of Penelope Driver, of Stanford University?"

"One of two sons. Fraternal twins. There's also a daughter."

"I know your mother. I gave a response to her paper at a conference in Rotterdam this past month."

"I'd forgotten. Penelope was in Rotterdam."

"You call your mother 'Penelope'?"

"I used to call her 'Penny' when we lived on Penny Lane."

Roseanne Phillip smiled quizzically at me. Sheila's father was intent on his chicken. He methodically cut off a piece of breast and lifted it on his fork.

"What kind of response did you give?" Sheila asked, passing the bread. "Were there a lot of people?"

"Several hundred. We were discussing female archetypes. You have to understand that Freddie's mother is something of a celebrity. And her work is highly controversial. She said that there were two main archetypes for women during the Christian Era, the Madonna and the Whore. And she argued that the Whore had triumphed. That we had completed the transition from Christendom to Whoredom. She described the change as part of a necessary historical process."

Roseanne knitted her brow and sipped her lemonade.

"I argued that the Madonna and the Whore represent a necessary choice to every woman. It is not just a matter of history or religion. It is a matter of biology and human nature. Every woman must face it."

She glanced at Sheila, who adjusted her napkin. I chopped at my asparagus with a knife.

"What do you think, Freddie?" Ben asked.

Irked by Roseanne's starchy posture, I was wondering if she and my mother hated each other. Of course they did.

"I really don't know."

"You mean you didn't come here expecting to be surveyed on your mother's ideas?" he said.

"To tell you the truth, what were they talking about, the Madonna and the Whore? No one's completely one or the other."

Ben Corcoran looked at me like I was a reasonable person.

"Except Madonna, who's just a whore," I added, for good measure.

"So you don't agree with your mother?" Roseanne said.

Sheila touched my hand. She coaxed me along with one of those admiring looks, you know, the kind patented by princesses long ago, to oblige the zealous suitor to slay the dragon, resurrect the kingdom, and if necessary swim the seven seas with a codfish in his mouth.

"All I'm saying is you have to do the best you can. If you screw up, you have to try to do better next time."

"It is always so interesting," Roseanne said, "to think of how a child develops in relation to its mother."

"Roseanne!" Sheila objected.

"We have the most delicious mangoes for dessert," Ben announced, drawing a curtain across the Elysian Fields of psychology. "I picked them up at the new co-op. I had never tried mangoes."

He smiled at his daughter. Between them they restored the atmosphere of the room to one of affectionate good humor matching the brilliant sunshine in the garden.

"They're wonderful," he told her. "Cool and delicious."

"Daddy's first mango," the daughter teased.

Over dessert we took up the topic of Iraq and the theory of just war. Ben thought it refreshing to see an old tradition shaping the debate. Just war theory was one of those rare holdovers from the Middle Ages that enjoyed success in modern times. He found it difficult, however, to judge whether an invasion of Iraq would be just.

"I will defer for now to the wisdom of the state," he said, adding upon reflection, "If the phrase is not an oxymoron."

Roseanne asserted with considerable heat that we had no business in Iraq.

"I will give you *auctoritatis principis*, since the blackguards in the Senate are likely to go along with it. But short of pernicious casuistry I cannot make my way to *justa causa* or *recta intentio*. We are neither advancing good nor avoiding evil."

"Care for another mango?" Ben said.

Roseanne went on to say we could kill Saddam tomorrow and some other monster would immediately take his place. I didn't catch her drift about Bush, the Israelis, and 9/11, though Ben apparently disagreed with her. Too many crashing cymbals.

Sheila feared the attempt to rebuild Iraq might backfire on us, even if it was undertaken for some good reasons.

"It's pretty small, the area where any of us can do some good in the world. Our own motives are mixed and things by their nature resist our control."

"Well," her father replied, looking at me in a friendly if undecided fashion, "one of those slender areas, I like to flatter myself, is my study. Why don't you come up and have a look at it?"

I trailed him like a tethered goat. In his study a rocking chair sat in the sun. A couple of books rested on the carpet, with a black notebook and a glinting gold fountain pen. He lifted a massive Latin dictionary from the floor and placed it on a tripod by the rocker. The Pope's picture hung in a wooden frame on the wall behind him.

"Who's that?" I said.

"I'm a religious man, Freddie," he answered, turning to look at the picture with me. "I suppose it could be considered a weakness."

"Honestly, I'd like to believe God was the truth. Only not at the cost of reality."

"That's the question, isn't it? In what direction lies reality."

A wide shelf skirted the wall under the picture. It supported an impressive collection of model buildings. They were perfect constructions, meticulous in every detail, down to the last railing.

"Did you make these?"

"I'm afraid so. It might as well be ships or airplanes."

I stooped beside the shelf and examined the model of an apartment block that recently had gone up in the Pearl District. There were courtyards, gardens, and fountains but no glitter or insidious pastel. There were lamps and balconies to scale, making a lovely effect. When I praised his work he tapped his finger on another model and compared its staircase to an armadillo's nose.

"You know Sheila's mother was from New York."

"Really?"

"Her family immigrated from the west of Ireland. They were country people."

"I didn't know that. I think the Fontanes came from France. At least that's what my father says."

"Were you raised religious, if you don't mind my asking?"

"My father was Catholic. But he dropped it and my brother and I were never baptized. My sister was, though. She and her husband are Catholic. My mother says Christianity is for losers."

"She's has a point," he said dryly. "I hope you don't mind my asking how you feel about it."

"I know your daughter and the church are connected. I respect that. But the church, what I've seen of it–I mean aside from all the corruption and the bad priests–it can seem out of touch with life. You can't house reality."

"That's a good way of putting it," he said, looking out the window. "The best houses don't pretend to be something they're not."

I heard a classical piano from downstairs. At first I thought it was a recording; then I realized it was someone in the house. The bass made a strong steady counterpoint as the treble ran off mathematically precise but melancholy phrases. Ben stood gazing at a tree in the backyard. It rose high above the lawn and I gradually saw that the leaves on its very highest branches were edged with yellow. He identified it as an oak. They were trying to save it.

When we left the house father and daughter lingered a moment on the path going over some business, which concerned the state of repairs in a parish building. Then she kissed him goodbye.

"I'll call you from Los Angeles," she said.

That Monday I received a letter from Jack. He'd written me care of Sheila. As she organized her things I sat down and read what he had to say:

July 22

Dear Rock Star,

Well I just heard Rex and The Brains on the radio in North Carolina. Quite a punchy little number.

I'm here at Fort Bragg with the 82nd Airborne Division. I'm on the crew of something called a Kiowa helicopter. It's a seven-man crew with two pilots. We carry two Hellfire laser-guided missiles, seven 2.75-inch rockets and a .50 caliber machine gun. You guys should have one on tour.

There's a lot of discipline here but I feel it's good for me. Tell the truth, I think it's saving my life. The men are good soldiers. Our Kiowa group is called the Wolfpack. You can tell we're going to stick together if the call comes.

I figure either you're dead of the clap by now or you're dating Sheila.

Love, Jack

EIGHT
LA

"F. U. I Just Want To Get My Rocks Off" continued its breathless climb up the charts. We shot the video and Crocodile got it into rotation the next week. The director spliced some footage of the band loitering around Compton onto a cartoon strip of a mutt named Rex who wore a red basketball jersey with a black number 1. Rex was the kind of mutt who walks on two legs, winks at the camera, and chain smokes. He exuded an air of disdainful boredom as he shuffled through the canine ghetto. In the street were dogs sniffing other dogs, dogs snarling and fighting, rutting poodles, a pit bull pimping by a mailbox, and a rottweiler in sunglasses tearing at a man's trouser leg. Rex the mutt bore a canine likeness to my brother, who had never been in a ghetto in his life. Hank appeared as a German shepherd banging on a trash can lid. I think the rottweiler was supposed to be me.

During the mindless chorus the dogs would rally together to rebuff the politicians trying to enter the ghetto. Bush tried and failed, then Blair, then Hillary, and then Hitler appeared, only to receive exactly the same treatment as Bush.

> F. U. I just want to get my rocks off
> Be cool, I'm Iraqi and I'm box office
> Old school, with a supermodel in my Lexus

Rex the man started cross-dressing. When he took the stage at the Staples Center in a red leather jacket, a pleated blue skirt, and white go-go boots the audience cheered like Romans at the circus.

He peeled off the jacket just before the big hit, unveiling a red basketball jersey with a black number 1.

"This next song isn't going to quit...," Rex announced as Hank started up the bass drum.

It was like some great liberation was at hand. Saddam was coming to save the world. Hollywood was his new capital. Institutionalized racism was being wiped off the face of the earth.

"...Because it's like my...It's like my...It's like my..."

Each time he said these magic words he pumped his groin in a show of raw machismo. The males responded by thrusting fists into the air and screaming. The females screamed even louder. When some young gentlemen from the lower mezzanine started diving into an impromptu mosh pit the police scrambled up the stairs to stop them.

> *F. U. I just want to get my rocks off*
> *Be cool, I'm Iraqi and I'm box office*
> *Old school, with a supermodel in my Lexus*

Afterwards I was joined backstage by Sheila and my brother-in-law. Sheila wore a sleeveless dress, which I believe she picked up second-hand. It wasn't a flashy dress, but it was shapely and elegant. She had a sense of humor that way, and she knew how to make an entrance. The dark cloth put her beauty in a new light, or an old light for that matter, like a lost vision from some forgotten romance. She wore her hair up, as when I'd first laid eyes on her.

"Who the fuck does she think she is?" somebody said.

Manny shook hands with Rex, who visited San Bernardino for the first time only the day before. He dashed over in his yellow Maserati, escorted by a porno actress named Nefertiti. She bedecked her weird body with bronze and silver that tinkled when she walked. Ellen and Manny seemed oblivious, but Sheila picked up the scent right away.

"I wonder if she does lesbian scenes," she said.

"You interested?"

"I could have 'Mantica for Congress' tattooed on my butt."

Over at the house Rex wrote the campaign a big check. He took several calls and referred frequently to his "career." The kids must have sensed he was preoccupied and ignored him. They didn't go near Nefertiti.

I briefly caught sight of Hank after the show. He was drinking a Perrier and talking to some friends. The truth is we'd left him to his own devices, and he found a way to survive.

LA is a city where bands that can sell out stadiums play night-clubs on occasion just to reconnect with an audience. It so happened that one evening Hank caught one of the best bands in the country at a Hollywood bar. The musicians in this band acquit themselves extremely well on their instruments. What is even rarer, they enjoy each other's company. Hank descended on Hollywood Boulevard wearing his emerald zoot suit. Just how he compassed its arrival in LA, I don't know. When someone introduced him at the club the band invited the young upstart to sit in on the traps. Well, Hank can actually play the traps. They put him on the spot with a drum solo, probably intending to show the kid up, and he earned a standing ovation.

Hank made friends with the drummer, a session player also named Hank, a childless man in his fifties. He and his wife, Sissie, practically adopted our boy. They showed him the town. They took him to baseball games and went snorkeling. Sheila and I joined them at a barbecue where Hank presided over the grill. He stood in the middle of the group wearing a blue apron with a black and white cow on it. I told him it was Cowman's cape and he needed to return it. But people looked surprised when I called him "Hank." Among his new friends he was simply known as "Junior."

The *LA Daily News* called Crocodile to arrange an interview. At first I didn't understand. A woman named Mimi Huang wanted to in-terview me by myself. She was doing a series for the *Daily News* on popular lyrics. I ended up speaking with her personally and invit-ing her over to the house.

It was a fine summer day when she rang the doorbell at exactly 3:00 pm. I took her out to the deck and we drank iced tea. She wore slender rimless glasses, a lime silk blouse with a frill, and a white miniskirt. Her dark hair was pushed back in a bun. She was easy going and a pleasure to look at. Readying her notebook she turned on a tape recorder.

"So, what do you like to do for fun?"

"I surf and collect stamps."

"All right. Who's the main influence on your writing?"

"My brother."

"Name a band or musician you hate."

"Only one?"

"Just one."

"R.E.M."

"Why?"

"Whenever I hear their music I want to set myself on fire and run down the street...Can you use the word *suck* in the newspaper?"

"Sure," she glanced at her notes and continued.

"Describe the rock and roll lifestyle in one word."

"It sucks."

"One word."

"Sucky."

"What do you think of being a celebrity?"

"It sucks."

"Please, Freddie. Your lyrics have a literary quality. Do you ever read books?"

"If I'm interested in a book I find somebody who's read it and ask them about it."

"But didn't you go to college?"

"I was an English major in college. You know, it was all theory."

"Come on."

"I've been reading a few fairy tales."

"What, you mean gay literature?"

"I mean fairy tales. 'Beauty and the Beast.'"

She regarded the cross and the Marian medal around my neck. Half the people you meet in LA wear crosses around their necks. The whores in LA wear crosses. Maybe it's so their johns won't fuck them in the ass.

"You're not really religious, are you?"

"I'm attracted to religion. I go to church sometimes, if that's what you mean."

"What church?"

"Roman Catholic."

"Do you believe in original sin?"

"It would explain a lot of things, wouldn't it? I mean, sin isn't just what other people do. Do I believe in original sin? I'd say it's a very democratic view of life."

"But your lyrics are completely nihilistic, Freddie. There's nothing pious about any of them. You're the man who wrote 'F. U. I Just Want To Get My Rocks Off.'"

I smiled. It was currently in the Top Ten.

"Well, Mimi, it's like a satire without any normal people."

Suddenly she turned off her tape recorder and said, "Didn't you go to Stanford University?"

"I graduated two years ago."

"So did I. I thought you looked familiar. I majored in Physics."

"Physics? What the hell are you doing here?"

"I took a leave of absence and got married. I had to get out of the lab. I'd been there since seventh grade."

"The kids want to come out and play," I observed, seeing a row of young faces squished up against the sliding glass door. "Should we let them?"

"By all means."

Julia, Ramon, and Carmen came crashing onto the lawn. Somewhere in an unfinishable conversation Ellen and Sheila followed them.

"I need to ask you questions about specific lyrics. Okay? "'Painkiller.'"

"I had a chronic headache when I wrote that. Later I learned it was dehydration."

"'Wire Monkey.'"

"It's about that famous experiment they did with the monkeys. There were some baby monkeys. A man in a lab coat took away their mothers and provided surrogates. He gave some of the baby monkeys a cloth monkey and he gave the other baby monkeys a wire monkey. The ones that got the wire monkey ended up, you know, slackers. But later they turned cannibal and ate the guy."

"'Jig.'"

"It's about a girl who had an abortion."

"What about the Hemingway reference? Do you read a lot of Hemingway?"

"Hemingway? I didn't know she was an author."

"The lyric makes it sounds like you get a kick out of abortion."

"I think abortion is evil."

"You really want me to print that? You think it's evil."

"As bad as Saddam."

The interview ended and I walked her out. We shook hands in a friendly way. As we stood in the open door, my brother-in-law pulled up in his Chevy sedan. He grabbed his brief case, closed the car door with his knee, sidestepped a tricycle, and put his cell away.

"Isn't that Emmanuel Mantica, the politician?"

"This is his house."

"His house?..."

"Wait a minute. I'll introduce you. He's a good guy."

"Aren't you Fred Huang's wife?" he asked, shaking her hand and grinning his politician's grin.

"Who's Fred Huang?" I asked as she drove off.

"He's the editor of the *LA Daily News*. It's a respectable paper."

The story ran on the cover of the Entertainment section. There was a picture of me dressed in black with the caption "F. Fontane." They printed the interview along with the words to "Jig," "Painkiller," and "Wire Monkey." Mimi said people over forty would find it difficult to understand me.

After the interview the A & R staff at Crocodile had their hands full. I spent hours sorting through stacks of letters and printed emails. Among the professional invitations was one asking me to speak on a panel entitled "The Sounds of Late-Capitalist Metanarrative: Popular Lyrics and the Death of Song." A primatologist named Lila wanted me to meet her monkeys. There was a group called ENERGY (Encouraging New Evolutionary Reform and Godliness in Youth) whose request went unanswered; when they kept leaving messages I took to calling them ENIGMA (Encouraging Nihilism In God, Man, and Animal). Judging that a priest had a special claim to my attention, however, I phoned Father Desmond Blair and agreed to meet him at a coffee bar.

I expected black clericals and a Roman collar; but here was a vibrant looking middle-aged man in jeans, an Italian sports coat, and a polo shirt. He wore his hair short and his beard neatly trimmed. He appeared to be a well-heeled member of the actor's union. Surrounding us at the bar a hundred gadgets with ten thousand buttons sent a million signals opening and closing the portals of virtual reality. Father Blair's first comment spoke to these surroundings.

"It's all going to change," he said, waving his soft white hand like a conjurer. "We've been living in a dream. People are going to look back in twenty years and wonder how they managed to hide from reality."

"I know what you mean. It's everything. It's the way we live."

He smiled like someone sharing an inside joke.

"We've traded the creed for credit, reality for virtual reality, parents for appearances. You can hear the crash coming like a tidal wave...Please call me Desmond," he concluded, as we exchanged a cordial handshake.

Over iced cappuccinos and biscotti we discussed the unreality of it all. He referred to the city as "La-La Land." When I asked him why he lived there, he ruminated on his work in the barrio. Unfortunately he no longer believed much could be done. The state had run out of money, and the America of Roosevelt and Kennedy meant nothing to an immigrant who'd made the border-crossing in an unventilated trailer last month. The gangs outnumbered the cops. Automatic weapons fell into the hands of whoever wanted them. Boys of thirteen would kill you for looking them in the eye. He shrugged a slender shoulder and said the city would probably go down in flames.

"We can talk about this some more. Why don't you join me for supper over at a friend's house? They're good people, albeit wealthy as hell. They do a lot of good for the city. We can go for a swim and relax."

We produced our cells and made a pair of calls. Minutes later we were driving into Laurel Canyon in a white Mercedez coupe. It was brand new. The top was down and the posh interior was cooling off as we broke free of traffic. It wasn't really his car, Desmond Blair explained. It belonged to the Aulettes, the couple I was going to meet. With their typical largesse they practically had given it to him. We passed a derelict church and he mentioned that the archdiocese stood on the brink of ruin. He blamed much of the trouble on John Paul II, one of the worst popes in all history so far as he was concerned. The American Church needed to go its own way or become extinct. He could recommend several excellent books on the subject. His mind brooded over collapse like a bird over a sinking ship.

He zipped smartly onto a private drive, waved a card at an electric gate, and whisked us up to a mansion of glass flanked by palm trees. At the door we were met by an elderly butler who received the priest on friendly terms. The butler led us out to a veranda, overlooking a spacious pool, where two men and a woman in a light summer dress rose from wicker chairs to greet us. A touch of drowsiness clung like honey to my senses as Desmond introduced Kim and Donna Aulette. The younger man, thin and good-looking, I took to be their son; but Kim Aulette introduced him as their friend Pete James.

Donna Aulette was a woman of considerable beauty. She kept a regal silence, with a pale forehead and raven hair like a heroine out of Poe. Her stately reserve drew moral support from the crucifix that hung from her neck. Kim Aulette was a vigorous fifty, muscular and trim, his thin hair fashionably cropped. He was a prince of finance, a shrewd profiteer who shared the opulence of his home with the same exacting forethought that overmastered his fellow businessmen.

Desmond Blair went to the bar and poured himself a drink as Kim Aulette asked me what I'd like. I said I'd take a martini straight up. He clapped his hands in approval and challenged Pete James to make me one. He was teaching Pete the fine art of mixology, he said.

"Do you work together?" I asked.

"Pete is my personal assistant."

I noticed Desmond Blair holding Donna Aulette's hand.

"Pete's a good egg," he said, more to her than to anyone else.

Pete James handed me a gin martini straight up with the fattest olive I've ever seen in my life. I pronounced it to be absolutely perfect. Then Kim Aulette applauded once again and he and Pete took their seats.

Desmond Blair related how the Aulettes had performed countless acts of charity for the parish. They'd saved the school where

Desmond was working, built baseball diamonds and basketball courts, and restored one of the crumbling Spanish missions.

"Millions and millions of dollars," Desmond Blair said, but Kim Aulette waved it off.

"I wish I could do more," he said. "Of course, I worry it's money wasted under the current regime."

"Bush...?"

"The Supreme Pontiff," Desmond Blair corrected me. "He's just a tyrant, really. He and a few henchmen have destroyed Vatican II. He's undone a lot of progress. Just when the church seemed poised to move forward, to leave behind the shadows and superstitions of the past. And the pain he inflicts with his devotion to an out-of-date morality..."

"A sad anachronism," Kim Aulette said.

I said, "Do you believe in sin?"

"Of course," Kim Aulette said, and the others nodded their heads in agreement.

"But it must be understood fairly," Desmond Blair said. "The real point is that we all sin. Straight people, gay people, married couples, bishops, popes, and priests. You can't impose artificial rules. You have to deal with each individual in a spirit of equality. For me that's what the Holy Spirit is all about."

The priest invited me to look around him, as if for visible confirmation of his remarks. I saw a pair of tall palm trees that rose indolently beyond the deep end of the swimming pool.

It's a lovely place," I said politely.

"It's very simple," Desmond Blair said. "There are three things we need in the church. Women priests, full recognition of homosexuals–I mean my God–and lay people in positions of power. The Pope should be a benevolent figurehead, not an aging fascist."

Donna Aulette was watching me. I admired the queenly sorrow of her face and the generous curve of her bosom.

"It's time for a swim," Pete James said, shepherding us.

He showed me to the bathhouse where he found a pair of baggy trunks for me to wear. They were covered with palm trees. I stepped into the pool and the warm water did nothing to dispel the monotonous languor that had pierced my spirit all afternoon. Kim Aulette swam gracefully over, barely rippling the water.

"I don't want to embarrass you, Freddie. But you remind us of our son."

"Your son?"

"Our late son. He passed away five years ago last March. It was drugs, Freddie. He was a musician like you. We were all together last week, Pete and I, Donna and Desmond, and I was reading the fascinating interview in the paper you gave, and it struck me how much you looked like Tommy. And then it sounded like you might be Catholic and I told Desmond that I would like to meet you and he arranged it."

"Oh."

"I think Donna saw the likeness between you and Tommy as soon as you came in. She wasn't expecting it, Freddie. Of course if there's anyone can comfort her, it's Desmond."

He stood in the pool up to his neck, his chiseled features like a Roman bust above the blue water. Pete James executed a swan dive as I lounged along the side, douching the muscles of my back.

"People have a right to be happy," I said.

The head emoted satisfaction.

"Thank God you're on our side. People can be so beastly. I mean, you expect it in business. But some things have to be sacred."

"There's just one thing I don't understand. Why don't you join another church? Why stay with Catholicism if it offends you?"

"Ah, Freddie. Life is so short. We don't have time to be hopping around from one communion to the other. If God is going to send me to Hell, so be it. I think he'll let me out eventually. Eternity's such a very long time."

I submerged myself and kicked like a frog across the width of the pool. When I came up for air Donna Aulette was telling us that supper would be served in half-an-hour. She smiled ambiguously and asked if I liked to swim.

At dinner she flattered me, praising my mastery of minor topics, hip-hop, the art of tattoos, the political future of California. She complimented my music as Mexican servants came and went with salads and breads and good Italian wine. Smiles flashed like money in the glow of laughter as the meal passed with the warmth of a tropical daydream. Amidst the musical conversation only some slight clumsiness on the servants' part occasioned a chord of tolerant murmuring.

Eventually I rose to go.

"Could someone please take me home?"

It was a phrase that, whatever its sources in my past, sank to the depth of my feeling, was saturated, transformed there–children do best with two loving parents–and brought up into memory again. A driver appeared and returned me to San Bernardino.

When Congress voted for military action in Iraq I could sense the political divisions in the country widening. People loved or hated the President with emotions that infected how they judged their neighbors. After months of politics I began to wonder if ignorance was the only solution. The rancor over judicial appointments, the angry tribute to the late Senator from Minnesota, the President's redneck manner, the passionate question of gay marriage, turned much of the campaign into a sophisticated brawl. The United States of America still existed as a geographical expression, but its future as a way of life was growing dim.

At the instigation of Manny's campaign manager, a clever dog named Bill Sikarski, Sheila and I spent a number of sunny after-noons handing people leaflets, buttons, and bumper stickers. Bill Sikarski liked sending us out on these missions because we looked "hip."

"You kids look hip," he'd say. "Let's get you back on the trail."

"I hate the trail."

"Come on, Fred. I've seen you out there. You do a fine job."

"But Bill, I don't know diddle about politics."

"Just work the crowd, son. Smile and work the crowd."

Sheila enjoyed herself. She joined in earnest conversations. She was a natural politician. The style I developed was to let her do the talking. If someone asked a question about policy, I referred it specifically to her.

We were at a community college before a highly trumpeted de-bate on abortion rights. We'd worked through a heap of campaign paraphernalia when Mimi Huang saw me and stopped to say hello. She was covering the event for the newspaper.

"I can't believe you're involved in politics," she said.

"Why not?" I replied, feigning surprise. "I'm a serious per-son."

"You're not here alone, are you?"

"Actually, I'm here with my girlfriend."

"You have a girlfriend?"

"Mimi, I have a *serious* girlfriend."

Sheila returned presently, and Mimi invited us to join her in the front row, which was reserved for the press. I hesitated. Though they seemed predisposed to like each other, it was unclear where Mimi stood on the abortion issue. I knew Sheila had strong feelings about it.

"We'd love to," she said. "It's nice of you to ask."

We bagged the campaign gear and took our seats among the representatives of the press. Looking around I observed a blind man with an enormous hairy dog, which met my gaze, a pair of stoical security guards, a group of German tourists talking very loudly in English, and, almost directly behind me, a baby fast asleep in a Moses basket. Several TV crews were filming the event, and the big hall bristled with lights and microphones. On stage the opposing camps sat behind linen-draped tables, stocked with pens, paper, and twelve-ounce plastic water bottles. Two young women occupied the pro-life table with a white-haired grandmotherly type. At the pro-choice table sat a triad of women in their fifties or early sixties. Their bloodless complexion and impassive demeanor reminded me of the gray women in the myth, who pass a single eyeball between them and stare at the frozen, mist-laden confines of the world. The moderator, a fat and goosey Meryl Streep look-alike, clung to the lectern in a baggy brown suit.

The first part of the debate bored the audience. There was too much technical information. It had to do with when a baby is conceived. Apparently it is impossible to pinpoint the moment of conception. So you can't say the soul enters the body at a specific moment in time. The pro-life side conceded the point; but the grandmother argued that the soul enters the body whenever a human being takes root.

"But how can you possibly tell when a human being takes root?"

"I can't tell," the grandmother said. "But you can't tell either. And that's my point, if you could hear it."

Getting into the act the audience variously cheered and booed at this riposte, so that the moderator had to remind them to please be civil. She told a joke about how you can tell a fascist from a communist in the dark, which the Germans thought very funny. Then she ticked off a long set of questions about parental involvement requirements, mandatory counseling and waiting periods, and whether the public should fund abortion clinics. The two groups haggled about "reproductive freedom," the pro-choice table insisting that even a twelve-year-old girl should have access to abortion on demand, since sex was just a fact of life. And though they were gray women speaking a gray language, with gray smiles and gray scowls, yet their underlying passions were savage and their intellects were sharp as knives. It was like watching a continent split in half, so vast a gulf of disagreement opened between the two sides. I almost expected a physical law of repulsion to assert itself and push the two tables into the wings. Since neither side could possibly persuade the other of anything at all, the prevailing strategy seemed to be to hold on until your opponent tumbled into the abyss of some extreme, unpalatable view.

One of the young women made an emotional plea against the technique known as "partial-birth" abortion, which involves drilling a hole in the baby's skull and actually sucking its brains out. Then they dismember it. The other side fired back with "the right of a woman to determine her childbearing." Fetal rights, by contrast, were a deception, a cynical strategy to whittle away at *Roe v. Wade*. A fetus has no rights. Future generations would simply accept that, by the just measure of objective development, a one-year-old chimpanzee has more right to life than a human fetus.

As if awaking from a nightmare the baby in the Moses basket started to cry. Its shrill repeated wail had a singular scraping effect, shredding the nerves like a dull razor. It only began to settle down when the grandmother, addressing the topic of abortion in the third trimester, declared that fetuses are not unfeeling jelly. She recalled how when her daughter gave birth to her first child, a girl named Cecilia, the newborn turned straight to her father upon hearing his voice, though the doctor and the nurses were all men. Cecilia must have recognized her father's voice from her time in the womb. One of the young women spoke to the point about chimpanzees. She said that to forget the difference between babies and chimpanzees is like forgetting you need a mother to love you, with human milk and human smiles, or you will never notice the difference between babies and chimpanzees.

The audience roared and railed and Meryl Streep struggled to maintain order. The pro-choice side stood firm. There were many important reasons to abort a fetus on the verge of nativity, nor should it be granted that a newborn was essentially different from a fetus. Higher primates take time to develop because of the size of their brains, and our species takes an especially long time before anything like personality emerges. The baby started whimpering. Moreover, any attempt to limit reproductive rights was simply an intrusion by the government where it did not belong. Only women bore children. Only women could be responsible for when and if they were born. In a nation free of theocrats and their nursemaids, it was a democratic principle.

Clutching its mother's breast as if for dear life the little infant howled and foamed like a mini-hurricane. It only subsided gradually, gasping in piteously long drawn-out breaths, when one of the young women remarked that third-term abortion "constituted murder most foul." You can judge a society, she said, by its treatment of the truly helpless.

"Don't talk to me of rights," she continued. "Our society is sacrificing millions of unborn lives on the altar of money, politics, and pride. And I don't include–because I can't calculate–the mental suffering, the untold anguish, the extreme forms of psychosis, experienced by women who have aborted their babies and later regretted the act. For society to be neutral before such evil is deplorable, for government to promote it is a descent into Hell.

"You may have heard of Hannibal, the famous Carthaginian general who led his army over the Alps and almost destroyed Rome. Carthage was a huge commercial town whose citizens offered up their babies to their Lord, Baal. Hannibal means 'The Grace of Baal.' The less sophisticated Romans, devoted to their Lars and Penates, put an end to Hannibal. They salted the fields of Carthage because they hated the perversities of Baal.

"Today we are met with a similar threat. The Madonna and Child may no longer guard our civilization. There appears to be a change unfolding. There appear to be new gods. But though they masquerade as choices, or usurp the title of rights and principles, the new gods are ancient and terrible and without pity. They are the gods of death."

Dazed by the speaker's strange eloquence, or suddenly meditative, or silently shocked, the audience refrained from further outburst. The mother was rocking the baby gently back and forth: the storm had passed. But no sooner had the pro-choice women turned their collective gaze toward the future of *Doe v. Bolton*, than baby Moses exploded like Krakatoa.

I wondered why the mother hadn't done the courteous thing and removed her child. Maybe it was because she was seated in the middle of a long row that made it hard for her to extricate herself. Maybe the baby was normally tranquil. The mother must have been aware of the outraged glances and menacing glares, a veritable shower of abuse, which fell upon her from every corner of the crowded auditorium. In any case the pro-choicers were no longer gray. They were livid. While baby Moses was screaming bloody murder one of them confused the names "Roe" and "Doe" for the third time, corrected herself for the third time, and began pounding the table with her fist. Then she pointed a long bony finger at the woman with the baby.

"Would you please get that damn baby out of here?" she said.

At once a great change swept the audience. From rows of gaping mouths a unified gasp signaled the onrush of an emotional tide, like the parting of the Red Sea. The mother put baby Moses in its basket and hastened to go. Whether the baby cried or slept was impossible to tell, for the multitude roared with all its might, ready to burst the walls with the energy of political fission. Pharaoh's army and the Israelites jostled in the throes of history gone mad. Meryl Streep banged her gavel and then threw her arms up in despair, persuaded that she and two security guards were no match for a civil war. I grabbed Sheila, and she grabbed Mimi, and we slipped quickly out an exit. Mimi then called the police.

"I wonder if babies are evolving," I commented. "They have to know where their bread is buttered."

"Survival of the fittest," Sheila said.

"My God!" Mimi said.

We watched the police arrive, and when at last the indignant mob started to disperse we went out for coffee. Together Sheila and Mimi passed humorous judgment on the event. They seemed to be in perfect agreement. Still, for the first time in my life with Sheila, I felt a twinge of jealousy, not being the sole center of attention... What's that you say? "Men?" "How predictable?"

In a TV ad run by "The Council for Social Justice" a worried-sound-ing white woman droned gloomily behind grainy footage of Christ on the cross and Manny next to an American flag. She used *troubled* once and *troubling* twice. In a single thirty-second spot she also managed to squeeze in *bigotry, controversial, extreme, hate speech, mean-spirited, Religious Right, spewing, spouting,* and *warmonger.* The ad, which seemed a patchwork designed to fit its negative vocabu-lary, ended with a dental close-up of Manny as the woman asked, "What is this country coming to?"

Manny's opponent, a veteran of the Great Society named Big Jim Dodge, was a man of the people. He was a man who knew how Washington worked. He was a man who won election to Con-gress eighteen times. Movers and shakers flew in from New York, Washington, and Wyoming to show their support for Big Jim. Divas sparkled and movie stars glittered at his rallies. Prominent academ-ics, university presidents, and general raisers of consciousness em-braced Big Jim Dodge as one of their own.

On a warm October evening Sheila and I sat in the basement of the house with Ellen, Manny, and Bill Sikarski. Manny went over a new speech and the others offered criticisms. He was pragmatic in his politics: get rid of the pork, recognize failed policies, balance the budget. But his rhetoric needed softening. A paragraph on con-sumer debt worried Ellen, who persuaded him to delete the phrase "a generation of spendthrifts." During these sessions I offered no suggestions. My one suggestion, a campaign slogan, had been so roundly squashed that I hesitated ever to speak again. But I like the sound of it: "Vote for Mantica, or be an antique-a."

Bill Sikarski stood to take his leave and then abruptly turned his attention to me.

"Almost forgot to mention it. One of the newspapers has run a story linking you and Manny."

I studied the clipping he handed me. It was an editorial from a major LA newspaper.

"So if Manny's 'the Religious Right,' what am I?"

"Keep reading."

Puzzled by the last paragraph I read it aloud to the group.

"'It is to be feared that Mantica's brother-in-law has opened a dangerous territory, a political shadowland where the extreme far right meets the extreme far left. The French, who have experienced this kind of complex phenomenon, have a phrase for it: *Les extrêmes se touchent.* The extremes meet. Political and religious extremism appear to have met in the congressional campaign of Emmanuel Mantica.'"

"Extreme far right elements of the left wing!" Sheila cried, unloosing a peal of delicious laughter.

Ellen and Manny were laughing too and Bill Sikarski scratched his tired scalp.

I desperately wanted to sleep with Sheila. Watching her move, hearing the shades and colors of her voice, in the tides and scents of unsparing full-blooded life, I was entangled with her and constantly aroused. It got to be exhausting. When I complained bitterly of the condition known as "blue balls" she suggested we pray. It didn't help at all. No, that's not exactly fair. It helped as much as a snowflake in the middle of a Texas heat wave. After a session of heavy petting left me humid and humiliated we had a real quarrel. Later that night she knocked on my door in her pajamas. In her hand was a red ceramic bowl full of ice cubes.

"Chew on these," she said, still angry at me. "They're delicious."

She turned away. I tried an ice cube. Hard it was, and very cold.

So it was a pleasant distraction to have dinner with Fred and Mimi Huang. They invited us to their home in the hills of Bel Air, where we were greeted in vivacious good style. Fred Huang grinned at me and quipped that he should have worn black. His leather jacket was still at the dry cleaners, he said. Mimi Huang looked prettier and happier than ever. Observing her and Sheila, two beauties in the April of their prime, I began to wonder if black really was the most appropriate color for the evening.

In the living room I was instantly drawn to a magnificent landscape painting. The rich intricacy of trees, rocks, and clouds showed it to be Chinese. Two tiny figures stood on a knoll above an immense ravine with a small sloped roof behind them. Fred Huang said it was a landscape in moonlight by the thirteenth-century artist Ma Yuan. When I asked him if it was the original he smiled and said it was an heirloom.

He was thirty, broad-faced and handsome, the most gifted son of a prominent Chinese-American family. He and Mimi had a servant on hand, an old man who carried a tray of hors d'oeuvres into the living room with meticulous grace. Fred Huang spoke to him in Mandarin. At one point he tickled the old man's fancy.

"This is Chen," said Fred Huang with a hint of exasperated affection. "He came to this country before I was born. My father found him a job at the lousy fish market and helped bring his family across. Now he insists on repaying a kindness of my father's."

"Fred hires a strange maid," Mimi said, "but a good Chinese servant he is opposed to. The maid costs plenty and couldn't care less about us, of course, while Chen costs nothing and treats him like a prince. 'Therefore,' says honorable husband, 'it is time to get rid of Chen.'"

But Sheila caught the serious side of Chen's business and said, "What's the price of love?"

Fred Huang called out in Mandarin to his butler, who gave a sharp reply, like a knife sectioning a fish in several firm strokes.

"I asked him, Sheila. He says love is too expensive for Americans."

"Smart Chinaman," Mimi said.

After dinner the girls sat out by the pool to enjoy the night air and Chen brought them drinks. Fred and I returned to the living room, where he fetched a handsome bottle of whisky from the liquor cabinet, recommending I take it neat. He poured two glasses and pushed one across the coffee table to me. It was peaty and delicious.

"I find it curious," he began, "your comments in the paper."

"Why?"

"When I was a boy, my parents tried to keep a connection to China. They preached to us about custom and the ethical life, but to me it all seemed hopelessly out of date. Confucianism is dead in China, you know. It died with the last dynasty, in 1911. Hardly anyone practices it anymore.

"Six months ago," he put down his glass and continued, "my father passed away. My mother read us something just before he died. We were sitting in the hospital at two in the morning. May I recite it to you?"

"Please."

He spoke the lines in Mandarin and then in English.

> *The Sacred Mountain is falling,*
> *The beam is cracking,*
> *The wise man is fading away.*

"Well, that was written 2,500 years ago. I guess it's the same old story of the light going out."

"It sounds like he was a good man, your father."

"My father had a pretty low estimate of the human race."

"Did Confucius?"

"Yes. He thought that goodness was very hard to come by."

"Goodness *is* very hard to come by."

"Dad hated sham morality."

I felt the genial warmth of the liquor in my veins and yet it struck me for the thousandth time that my own father was worse than a failure. He was a coward before the great questions of life. Failures by the world's standards may have something to show in the end, after all.

I said, "The only thing worse is no morality."

"I've been thinking about the future of the country. I agree that we need social services. Big government is to some extent necessary–I'm not a libertarian. But we can't all be wards of the state. There comes a point...ethics, art, love, the good life, they begin at home, with the family."

"I agree. But good fathers are hard to find."

"I'm just an echo of mine," he said, and tugged his lip so that somehow I shared his emotion.

The women returned in their loveliness. Mimi put on some opera and we replenished our drinks. Fred delighted me by joining in with the lead tenor. He barked out one of the arias in Italian, as Sheila and I waltzed around the room, lifted by a glad passion that delivered us from sorrow like a rose from its thorns. Chen bid us all goodnight and the party didn't break up until dawn. It was the beginning of a long friendship.

The Sunday before the election a surprising editorial appeared in the *LA Daily News*. Alongside several endorsements for candidates from the other party, the paper had come out in support of Emmanuel Mantica. The writer argued that the campaign against Mantica had become too bitterly partisan. Good men and women belonged to either party. We should recognize signs of outstanding character across political boundaries. Emmanuel Mantica had waged a fair and honorable campaign. His clarity on the issues reflected his commitment to the democratic process. The *Daily News* was endorsing Emmanuel Mantica for US Congress.

NINE
The Contract

Randy Pace finished talking to his secretary over the intercom. She sounded tense and overworked. From his end of the conversation I judged he was scheduling a class of some kind.

"That's my alma mater," he explained. "Once a year I drive up there and meet with students who are going into business. Joe Cobb, the CEO of Crocodile, is also an alum. In fact they're naming the new chapel after him–that's something else I need to schedule."

He pressed a button.

"Britney, don't forget to pencil in that chapel business."

"All right, Mr. Pace."

"Between his money and my seminars," Randy Pace confided, "I tell you Crocodile practically runs the place."

Then he said it was time to get to work. The Company had invested some real capital and he freely admitted it was paying off. He'd had a hand himself in pushing the deal through with the higher ups.

"You mean Reverend Cobb," I said.

It was the Monday before Election Day and we were seated in the boardroom of the Crocodile Building. A cherry table, thick with lacquer, caught Randy Pace's reflection and seemed to magnify it upside down. Gold and platinum records gleamed from the sun-lit walls. Green Crocodile coffee mugs populated the table, green Crocodile pencils played in our hands, and directly opposite me hung a life-size cartoon of a green carnivorous lizard.

"Tell you the truth, you should be glad I'm reminding you, very gently of course, of your contractual obligation. You need to think about your career and believe me, the best thing, the very smartest thing you can do right now, is to strike while the iron is hot."

"Funny, I never understood that expression."

"I'm saying you have to stay the course."

"Not change horses in midstream."

"I'm saying Rex and Freddie Fontane will be household names in a few years, if you can just keep your eye on the ball."

"Stick to the game plan."

"Exactly."

"Get with the program."

"What about me?" Hank said.

"You know what I mean, Hanky."

"Hanky?" said the least important member of Rex and The Brains. "Hanky is not acceptable."

"We're a good company, a reputable company, a fine, fine company let me tell you. Everything here's totally above board and all of us like all of you," he continued, seeming to ward off flies with his left hand. "I think you're the most talented young band we have. The first album's doing great. I love the new demo. As for that writer's block of yours, Freddie, you've just got to let it flow, man."

This burst of eloquence seemed to please him and he flashed his eyeteeth.

"Now I've asked John to book three weeks for you in a first-rate recording studio."

"It's all taken care of," Beazler said. "They start December 2nd."

Beazler was practically becoming Randy Pace, and I found the transformation fascinating. The novice adopted the master's moves: the sad-sack gaze, the knuckle cracking, the itchy catch in the voice. Beazler was losing weight, and Randy Pace was gaining hair. It was like something out of Dante.

"You'll finish by Christmas, take a great vacation, and we'll get you out on tour with a new CD by February. We'll supply excellent perks, I'll tell you that. We won't scrimp. You boys will be well provided for. And I'm sure there will be *whores galore.*"

"Sounds like an album title," Rex said.

I said, "Maybe for The Lords of the West."

"What's that?" Randy Pace asked.

"My old band," Beazler explained. "I taught Rex everything he knows. It was in Portland long ago. I found him on a streetcorner."

"What are you, his pimp?" I said.

"Fuck you, Freddie," Rex said.

"I'm sure things will improve as soon as the election is over," Beazler said diplomatically.

"Oh yes, the election," Randy Pace said. "I'd forgotten about that. Your brother-in-law, isn't that right? Tell you what, I'll write him a check. Is he going to win?"

At 8:00 pm on Election Day neither candidate was conceding. The national media picked up the story of the tight race. TV crews invaded the street with vans and satellite dishes. Manny's extended family joined us and when the lights and cameras barged in we must have had forty people in the house, four generations, with Manny, Ellen, and their children sitting on the living room sofa, the proverbial island in the storm. Twenty minutes later they were seated on the same sofa, watching themselves watch the news as the media storm intensified. Around midnight Manny bid his brothers, sisters, in-laws, nephews, nieces, parents, and grandparents goodnight. At 1:00 am he held a staff meeting. At 3:00 am we went to bed.

What happened next surprised everybody. Early in the morning I entered the house to find Bill Sikarski waving his hands like an orchestra conductor. Next to her husband Ellen had little Julia on her lap. She drank intently from her juice cup, absorbing the nervous energy like a funny little flower. Bill Sikarski was explaining that Manny had gone ahead two hours ago when the returns from the last ward came in. He held the lead by eleven votes. The margin was so slim that a recount was mandated by law.

Sheila had booked a flight back up to Portland for the following day. She needed to make some arrangements for graduate school. She was annoyed with me. She kept looking as if I was expected to say something. Then she raised the possibility of her having to stay in Portland.

"I need to do some things."

"Like what?"

"I haven't seen my father in months. I miss my friends. And I need a break. The campaign has worn us all out."

"These people love you, you know."

She glared at me.

"I suppose you're going to see that handsome young architect. What was his name? Eliot Buckley."

"What if I do see Eliot? He's a thoughtful person. You know, architects are artists too. They win prizes."

We started to squabble. We let the little devils have their way with us. They afford their mite of pleasure, don't they–the little devils? She wondered if she had given too much of herself, too easily. I called her an ice queen. It was such a stupid remark I was tempted to slap her.

"I didn't come down here to work on a *relationship*, Freddie."

"What the hell do you mean by that, Sheila?"

"Do you remember that night, before you left on the tour? You asked me why I knelt in church."

"What do you want me to do, kneel?"

"You don't understand. Sometimes you have to make peace."

"With what?"

"With how things are. With what's bigger than yourself."

"Right now that would appear to be Eminem."

"Aren't you getting sick of irony? I know I am."

"Sick to death."

That evening I went over the situation with Ellen. She listened carefully and then located her copy of the recording contract. She said my best hope was to make three or four successful albums and then go to court seeking a better deal. By that time we could plead we were very young when we started. We could imply Crocodile had entrapped us. It was true the contract was perfectly binding. But some judges look askance at music industry practices. Ten albums is a heavy burden to impose on a young band.

"Fuck off, God."

"Shut up, Freddie. You don't know what you're talking about."

She studied the contract again, searching for a way out. Then she ticked a small checkmark in the margin.

"That single of yours. How high is it on the charts?"

"It's number two."

"Do you think it might reach number one?"

"It's lost its bullet."

"Bullet?"

"That means it's expected to fade. Why?"

"Well, you see, I called one of my girlfriends from law school when I looked over your contract last spring. She's someone who does this kind of work. She told me I should stick in a few small provisions that might be useful down the road. The only item Crocodile let stand is this one, where I've just put a check. If any of your recordings go to number one, then you get to break the contract if you want to, which obviously you would want to do, and renegotiate the remainder of the contract. You'd even be free to deal with another company. It would be like starting over."

"So everything hinges on whether the dumbest single ever made goes to number one?"

"That would appear to be the case," she said, putting down her pencil.

"You're out of your mind," Rex said. "It's what we've wanted since we were twelve."

We were enjoying a steam bath at a celebrity gym called Dino's. Randy Pace had rewarded the Fontane brothers with membership cards and told me specifically to get some R and R. There were the usual things one would expect, barbells, jogging machines, saunas, jacuzzis, a swimming pool. Then there were a staff of Schwarzeneggers in red and buff uniforms, a liquor bar, a coffee bar, a sushi bar, a jewelry shop, a tech shop, an S-and-M parlor called "Liza's Buttique," and a very small very expensive hotel.

We sat on the top bench with our loins wrapped in thick cozy white towels. A sign on the back of the door said NO SEX IN THE STEAM BATH.

"You're a great singer and a great musician. I really mean that. But it isn't what I want to do with my life."

"Look, man, I've got the coke thing totally under control, if that's what you mean. You don't have to get addicted, you know. That's a fucking myth."

"What about the other stuff?"

"Like?"

"The porno actresses. What's that about?"

"What's wrong with porno? You know what your problem is, Freddie? You don't notice things. Most girls would love to get into porno, only they're too fat or too ugly or they can't afford to pay the plastic surgeon. I just gave a really nice girl some cash for implants."

"I see, you're in it for charity."

He raised his eyebrows and gave me a sad look. He didn't want to fight. He simply couldn't grasp my perspective.

"All I'm saying is it comes down to sex."

"And love?" I asked.

"It's an illusion!" he said, slapping my leg. "The only fact that counts is that some people are on top, maybe not the right people, but that's the way it is."

"And you're on top."

"We're on top. And women dig the power trip. It's human nature."

Dripping wet and laughing a pair of girls entered and spread out their white towels, dipping their dainty bottoms. They glanced up at us and smiled. They were topless.

"You bitches actresses?" Rex said casually.

It turned out they worked for Gus Hayes, a young man with a Princeton degree. Hayes had applied his cutting-edge entrepreneurial skills to the adult film industry and made a fortune. He was a visionary producer with a mission: to make porn as American as apple pie. Before long he'd be running for Senator from New Jersey.

"I'm friends with Gus," Rex said. "I was over at his mansion just the other day."

"Fucking everyone knows Gus," the actress said, the one who was doing the talking.

"So what have you been in?"

"Well, my latest is *The Twelve Whores of Christmas*. Get it? 'Ho-ho-ho.' It'll be out next week."

"Just in time for the holidays," he said. "How many have you done?"

"A fucking ton," she laughed. "I've been a busy girl."

She rattled off a few titles as if she was interviewing for a secretarial position and someone inquired into her computer skills. Meanwhile the other girl faced the conversation.

"What about you?" Rex asked her.

"I have a part in *Just Desserts*," she said with a southern accent. "It's Gus's newest film."

"You're a really hot girl. What's your name?"

"Sheryl," she said smiling.

"Come up here, Sheryl, and let's have a good look at you."

She banged up the steps in her thong and plastic clogs. Standing a foot below us she pulled her long wet hair back into a pony tail and pushed her chest out. She wore a thin ring of silver in her navel.

"Where are you from?" Rex asked with a grin.

"Decatur, Georgia. I'm a country girl."

"How long you been here?"

"Six months."

"How do you like it?"

"It's rougher than I expected."

"She can fucking take it," the other girl said. "She needs to loosen up, if you know what I mean."

"I'm thinking of quitting," Sheryl replied with a sulky look, "if they're not nicer to me."

Gus Hayes gave her the run of the gym for her trouble. It was in his interest to keep her in shape. He stocked the gym the way a sportsman stocks a lake.

"It's all about performance," Rex said.

"Damn straight," the other girl chimed in.

"Aren't you Rex Fontane?" Sheryl said.

"Tell your friend to come up here, Sheryl," Rex said.

"Velvet, come up here. It's Rex Fontane."

Velvet clattered up the steps and stood large as life before me. Her face was less attractive than her friend's. It was slightly pitted and she was older. Plus her tits were fake balloons, Sheryl's were natural teardrops.

"You guys are great," she said, patting her colleague's moneymaker. "They were just playing you in the gym."

"Thank you, Velvet," Rex said. "Now where are you from?"

"San Diego."

"Your nipples are hard," I said.

She smirked and looked me in the eye. Then she began to knead her tits, pinching her nipples and composing her face into a vacant leer. It must have been a reflex. Cool air rushed in as another girl jerked open the door, let out the steam, and went away.

"*Just Desserts*, huh?" Rex said, focusing on Sheryl. "I like it. What's on the menu?"

"Just about everything!" she exclaimed in a flight of nervous laughter, so that her accent slipped a little. "Gussie says we're competing with Europe...It's like an international competition or something."

"The Olympics of Sodomy," I suggested, thinking that Velvet would be pleased to be cornholed, right then and there.

"So you girls want to party?" Rex asked as the giggles died down.

"Definitely," Velvet said.

"Sheryl?"

"Are you going to be *awfully* mean?" she said.

"Yes," he said.

They laughed again and waited to see if we had anything more to offer.

"Thanks, girls," he said. "Why don't you go ahead and take a seat."

"Ouch! it's hot," Sheryl said, returning to her bench.

I said, "It's too fucked up."

"Save it, Freddie. It's human nature."

"You tell me you believe in God. Do you believe in sin?"

"I'll tell you something about sin, all right? Jesus Christ was a loser. They nailed him to a big piece of wood, he fucking died, and they buried him. People feed their fantasies but that's what happened."

"What if he rose again?"

"I can't believe you believe that crap."

"I don't, but what if he did?"

"Sheryl," he called, "do you believe Jesus rose from the dead?"

"He might have," she wondered.

"Sheryl, you want to see my dick rise from the dead?"

"Should we come back up?"

"You better wait a minute."

"Look, Rex, I'm just asking, what if he rose again? There were actually a lot of witnesses. Not all of them were country bump-kins."

"I am not a country bumpkin!" Sheryl protested.

"Let's blow this pop stand," Rex said at last, like he hadn't heard a word.

He gave Sheryl a kiss.

"I'll see you again," he said. "I like your style."

"Bye!" the bitches called after us.

I planned on seeing the Billboard charts before Sheila's arrival. But I overlooked the fact that Monday was Veteran's Day. The charts wouldn't be out until Tuesday. As the bizarre timing hit home the future seemed to cast a threatening shadow, like an ambush or a revelation from the lurking recesses of nightmare: it was the day Sheila was scheduled to return and the results of the recount were to be announced.

At Monday's rehearsal Rex was humorous and relaxed. He held to the conviction that I'd come around after the election. When I re-marked offhandedly that I was cracking up he put his arm around me.

"You and me both," he said.

Then he took the three of us out–me, Hank, and Beazler–for Chinese.

But I declined an invitation to hang out with him afterward. Oe-dipus Leech, lead singer of The Shame, lived a few doors down the hall from Rex's apartment. He and my brother ruled over a constant party where there were no hosts and no guests. Underage girls at all hours could be discovered loitering in the stairwells. Known lo-cally as "the leeches," they were perverted Barbies without a doll house. Oed and Rex had a list of pet names for them as well as their building, which they called "The Convent."

So I drove back alone to Ellen's, read Carmen a goodnight story about a knight, a dragon, and a princess, passed a few ironic com-ments that she wisely ignored, and cracked open a fly-green bottle of Kentucky bourbon. I proceeded to knock a pretty good hole in it, watching a movie about Hollywood actors who lie and screw and cheat one another until the last one's dead. Then I went to bed and jerked off.

The next morning I picked Sheila up in an LA drizzle. Right from the start we had trouble making conversation. The drive to the hotel lasted over an hour and the radio was full of nothing. She asked about the band and I gave her an account of the antics in the steam bath, including a graphic description of Velvet and Sheryl. Then I repeated Rex's theory of human nature. How people just want sex and power. It was a mean thing to do, and it brought an unexpected consequence. She said he was right. Sin was too strong. She'd been lying to herself.

"Why don't we just get a room at the hotel?" she said.

"Shut up."

"Come on, I want to. You can fuck me. Then I'll go to confession."

"Shut up, Sheila. You're not so innocent."

"I never said I was."

"Nobody is."

"Come on," she insisted, "I know exactly what you want."

"You do, huh?"

"And I know what I want," she said, staring out her window as the road went by. "I masturbated for hours last night. I love to sin."

"Good. We'll get a room."

"Good. We'll get this farce over with."

It was a big hotel. A hundred people crowded the lobby but there was no line at the registration desk. I booked the room and Sheila gave the clerk her Visa card. He asked if we had any baggage and wished us a nice day.

Rubbed raw and exhausted we walked away like prisoners. We were silent, our heads bowed in front of a tall bronze elevator door, when it opened and Ellen stepped briskly out.

"There you are!" she said.

Family and staff were expecting the count in one of the ballrooms. The candidate saw us come in and immediately gave Sheila an affectionate hug. Then he turned to introduce her to the head of the party's state committee.

"Jim, this is Sheila Corcoran, my brother-in-law's...?"

Manny was looking at me for a little guidance as the older man eyed the nubile beauty in the tight black jeans and rose blouse.

"My, uh, brother-in-law's friend."

"A pleasure."

"It's nice to meet you," she replied. "I think I recognize you from the campaign. Of course it all went by so quickly..."

"She was terrific!" Manny said. "She and Ellen are good friends."

A few minutes later Bill Sikarski arrived in his rumpled suit, beaming and flashing a V-sign. The room erupted in boisterous celebration. Balloons and confetti invaded the air. Kids leapt around in unconstrained joy. Manny slipped off and returned announcing that Jim Dodge had just called to congratulate him. People were floating like mystics on the sea of blue carpet, raising toasts, cheering and exulting.

Waving his speech Manny directed the family to the stage. In the squeeze and commotion I felt a surge of panic and Sheila and I were both reluctant to move. My will was ebbing from my body like a wall breaking down. We mounted the platform but stood far to one side as Manny took his place in the center. He thanked Ellen and Bill. Then he began to read his speech.

I didn't follow a word of it. The cameras were humming and Manny and Ellen delivered their parts right on cue. A siren wailed in the street like an abandoned infant. As it faded my thoughts returned to the movie of the night before. Lie, you handsome actors. Mouth your phony lines. Weave your faithless plot.

The sounds of the speech had split apart into nonsense when the last cadence died away and the ballroom applauded. They were happy now. They were many and loud and they clapped for a long time, creating an inhuman sound like rain exploding on a highway. I could hardly hear my cell jingling above the din.

It was Randy Pace.

"I have some good news for you, Freddie. We just found out and I wanted to call you myself. You have the number one single in the country. Congratulations. We're very proud of you."

I saw a clock in the glare. Then I put my arm around Sheila. It was by far the most warmth I'd shown her all day. She was trembling and pressed her body against mine.

"I quit."

"What's that, Freddie? What are you saying?" Randy Pace asked.

"I said I'm done. I quit. I'm quitting the band."

Ellen glanced over and saw me taking the call. She read my thoughts and put her hand to her mouth as I put the phone away. Sheila looked me in the eyes.

"Would you tell me what's going on?"

There was almost no time.

"Will you marry me?"

"Will I do what?"

"Will you marry me? I love you. I'm...proposing. Do you want me to kneel?"

She looked in a trance, breathing against my neck. She softly nuzzled my neck.

"What are you talking about?"

"Will you marry me?"

Time came flying back.

"Yes. I think I will. Yes."

Epilogue

Rex wouldn't even talk about the wedding. My leaving, he said, left him completely in the lurch. They had to try out a dozen bass players, pick one, make an album, and organize a tour. He said I was jealous of his success. I denied it, but I'm sure others agreed with him. For several months he and I stopped speaking altogether.

Crocodile re-signed him to a fat contract. He was going to call his new album *Wallop*, but the company overruled him. The theory in Marketing was that the target audience would have trouble with the word "wallop" because it was hard to spell. In the end *Rex Rox* shot into the top ten like a platinum rocket, another brilliant success for Luke Pound. Hank played drums and Harry of The Warts replaced me on bass. Beazler wrote the lyrics. They weren't as bad as I'd hoped.

We were printing out invitations about the time Rex was starting his tour. One night my phone rang at midnight. The caller sounded high.

"How's Little Miss Jesus?" he said.

"She said something about you."

"Little Miss Jesus?"

"She said you should be the best man."

There was a pause.

"Sorry, man," he said. "I got to go."

It was Penelope, of all people, who prevailed upon him to change his mind. She flew to Chicago, where he was in his second month of touring, bought him dinner, talked for hours, and at the last minute he relented. She chalked it up to fate.

"Fate?" I said to her on the telephone. "I've never heard you talk about fate."

"It's the topic of my new book," she said, sounding pleased with herself. "The publisher sent me an advance, you know. Academics usually don't get advances."

"Congratulations. What's it going to be this time?"

"*The Love of Fate*," she said. "I hold to the Nietzschean position. You have to be strong enough to love your fate."

I said, "What if you love the wrong fate? Like a drug addict who wrecks his life."

"Then let the chips fall where they may."

Adrian had dumped her for a graduate student in his seminar on Fanon and Foucault. The happy couple was living in Carmel-By-The-Sea.

"Of course it's a tragedy, from my point of view. I have the courage to say that.

"Because I had the will to love," she added. "Otherwise it wouldn't be tragic. Without the will to love it's simply the gross stupid absurdity of existence."

"I know what you mean."

I didn't exactly agree with her, but I could see her point of view.

Rex never answered our invitation. I knew he was coming because Penelope told me. He was bringing one of his girlfriends. The evening of the rehearsal he just appeared, a tall handsome man in black. He came striding down the aisle to where I was standing with Sheila and Brother John.

"Tell me what to do," he said, looking only at me.

I said, "Aren't you Rex Fontane?"

"No. That's my twin."

"But I'm your twin."

"Then it must be me."

"The ring," Brother John said gently. "Your job is to give him the ring."

Later that night, after the rehearsal dinner, Rex and I went out for a drink. We found a hole-in-the-wall in Old Town, a smoky dive where none of the seven customers recognized us, or if they did it had no discernible effect. A jukebox, hooped with yellow neon, was blasting Elvis as we entered.

"I got to meet Van Sligo last week," Rex began. "He invited me up to his hotel suite. It was just the two of us. We sat around drinking tequila and watching soccer.

"'There's success,' he tells me, 'and there's the days of your strength. And they're not always the same thing.' Then he dozes off with his boots on. So I settled him on the couch and shut the door behind me and left. It was weird. He was totally alone."

We were discussing the bitch goddess Fortune when Shreddy appeared: Ted Shred of The Zeros. It must have been his usual watering hole. The bartender grumbled his name in salute.

"We broke up," he soon explained. "Then we had The Torpedoes. But that ended too. Lately I'm just kind of on my own."

"Going solo?" I said.

"No. Not playing at all."

The papery color of his skin always amazed me. But now, in the dark yellow light of the bar, he looked absolutely ghostly, like a man about to make his final exit. His blond hair was white. His eyes seemed to float in a state of disembodiment. I recalled his heroin habit.

Rex rolled up Shreddy's sleeve and inspected his ravaged arm. It looked like a battlefield. He ran his finger over it.

"Holy shit, man," he said. "You don't have a fresh vein in your body."

"There's a couple left," Shreddy replied cavalierly, rolling the sleeve back down. "Just not in my arms."

"What are you going to do with your life, Shreddy? Where do you go from here?"

As Rex was talking I ordered another round with a glass for our guest.

"I don't know," Shreddy said. "Wherever fate takes me."

"Fate," I thought. "What a fuck job."

I raised my glass in a toast.

"Here's to hope."

One of the nighthawks at the bar heard me and raised his glass to no one in particular. Maybe he was hoping for a refill.

"Freddie believes in Jesus," Rex said. "You know: change your life, the grace of God."

"I don't mind Jesus," Shreddy said. "There's worse people in life...But there's a guy I need to meet, and he ain't Jesus."

"Here, man," Rex said, fumbling in his wallet for hundred dollar bills. "Take this."

"Shit," Shreddy said. "Well, thanks. I wish you luck on your career. See you later, Freddie."

Brother John married us on the last day of May. I had wanted a winter wedding, but it had to wait until the young pagan was baptized. And that had to wait until proper instruction took place. So I endured a season of celibacy.

It was a happy ceremony with family, friends, and numberless flowers. The bride wore her mother's wedding dress. What Ben Corcoran thought, I can hardly imagine. He seemed in another world, standing in a shaft of sunlight. Rex managed not to drop the ring, I managed to put it on Sheila's finger, and Brother John managed to smile on man and wife.

The reception featured an unexpected guest in the aging person of my father, the great Les. He was out of the slammer and back in the saddle again. He'd been able to track Rex down through the computer in the prison library. Now he awaited us with open arms. Among the smiling guests at their tables, and at the open bar, he made no secret of the fact that he'd been a sensational father, that he knew what was best for his boys, and that, in short, we owed it all to him.

"The boys' father," he said, shaking hands with all comers.

Gradually it tilted into a question.

"The boys' father?"

Don't misunderstand me. Les wasn't questioning himself. Far from it. He was congratulating himself. He was implying that no good and sane person could fail to recognize the bonds of loyalty, of devotion, of sacrificial love, that proclaimed his paternal standing in the eyes of a benevolent but scrupulous deity.

The phrase became a hook.

"The boys' father?"

It was a riddle for the ages, plucking from the bright spring air a note of theological mystery. And in fairness to the great Les, it must be said–magnanimous fellow–that he didn't expect anyone to measure up to his own selfless standards. He knew that people often deceive themselves. He observed how they persist in thinking they're on the side of the angels, no matter how great their iniquity, how evil their sin. He reminded his audience that even Satan was on the side of the angels. And though they were fallen angels, it didn't weigh in the scales of his (Satan's) judgment, because from his point of view it seemed so obvious that God was wrong.

They say the apple never falls far from the tree.

To make our family reunion complete my sister came from San Bernardino with Julia, Ramon, and Carmen. Manny flew from Washington to Portland, where he rendezvoused with her and the kids. I caught sight of Ellen and Penelope actually speaking, while the children danced around a giant of a man, Sheila's uncle it turned out, and the band accosted my ears with an Irish jig. Ellen was talking and Penelope was nodding her head. They didn't make any special progress, and Penelope still refuses to be called "grandma." But it was something to see them together.

Rex arrived at the reception with "Sheryl Lewinski," who was the hottest thing in porn. *Just Desserts* won her industry's top awards. It made millions of dollars and she herself took Best Newcomer (get it?) for her role as the scheming ingenue. She wore a low-cut blue dress, a smear of red lipstick, and breathed a greasy kiss on my cheek.

"Your wife looks so beautiful," she sighed in her accent of gossamer and moonshine.

"You look like a million bucks," I said.

Later I found her drunk and teary. She was confessing to Mrs. Gruda that her real name was Sue and she came from Seattle. Then Rex fetched her and they left.

I was delighted to clap eyes on Hank Freed. He soon laid my fears to rest. He knew how to handle himself on tour, especially now that he no longer had to avoid my bad example. John Beazler showed up in black tie. I forget if we invited him, but he wept during the ceremony. At the reception I saw him in the men's room.

"You want to do a line of blow?" he said.

I stared incredulously.

"Just kidding," he said. "But there goes your wedding present."

The Huangs flew up from LA and Mimi was pregnant. I saw

the Coves in a group with Mr. and Mrs. Gruda and their handsome youngest son, who was deep in conversation with Tim Cove's sister, Jennifer. On leave from the Army, Jack was resplendent in his Pfc dress uniform. He reminded me that he'd been fighting evil incarnate, all the while I was standing around moon-eyed over Sheila.

About this time I received a card from the world-famous artist Sharon O. All it said was "Hope you're happy." Sheila gazed at the painting on the card.

"What does it mean?" she asked.

The red bars and strange white letters suggested no ready explanation.

"It's a private language, I guess. She's kind of a priestess."

Sheila considered the painting a moment longer.

"Kiss me," she said.

I kissed her again and again as the card slid to the ground.

As for the facts of life, I like to think we can live with them. So let me reflect for just a moment on our wedding night.

Never mind!

Sheila timed it so that she was nine months pregnant at her graduation in Rome. She gave birth the next day, and we named the child Rose, after Sheila's mother.